ANGIE DEREK

Witch Light

Contents

Acknowledgement

Thank you to everyone who encouraged and helped in the creation of this book. A big thank you to my beta readers, Jaye Shields and Lisa Filipe, and my copy editor, Diane Noland.

Chapter 1

Lily Conner raced up the stairs. Her breath came in ragged gasps. The only thing keeping her moving was the vampires in hot pursuit behind them. The hotel lobby crawled with vampires blocking their escape. Unfortunately, two vamps had spotted them darting back up the fire stairs.

Her own personal vamp ran behind, keeping her going at a non-human speed and carrying her four-year-old sister. If she were holding Sophie, they wouldn't be moving at this hard pace.

"Faster!" Brenda pushed steadily against her back.

She didn't waste breath telling Brenda she couldn't go any faster. It didn't matter that they were being pursued. Her body could only run so fast. The sound of the other two vamps climbing a couple of stories below echoed up the stairs. Fighting against her growing fatigue, she somehow pulled the energy out to run up to the final floor of the high-rise hotel. She shoved against the fire door and stumbled into the large and extensive gym stretched out across the entire length of the hotel.

Staggering a few feet in, she collapsed against the soft gymnastic mats laid out in a large square in this corner of the room. On her knees, she sucked in air and pressed on her throbbing chest. The pain threatened to swamp her, but she pushed it down as oxygen struggled through her lungs. She glanced around the room to assess escape and weapon possibilities as Brenda had drilled her. Her backpack carried two stakes and a change of clothing. Her sister wore an identical if smaller backpack. But the problem with stakes was having to get up close and personal for them to be effective.

The main entrance across the room worried her the most. The double elevators could fit more than twenty vamps if they were on their way up. During the two years she had been on the run from the vampires she had learned that fighting a pack was practically impossible. You had to run and run fast.

Brenda set Sophie down next to Lily, her lightning-fast gaze taking in the room as she prepared for the two vampires. The vamp dropped a much larger duffle bag which held the rest of their possessions and her own personal backpack next to Lily.

Lily had to get her energy back if she was going to have any chance of defending herself and Sophie from the two vamps about to come through the door let alone the master vampire controlling the vamp mob pursuing them. The pack wouldn't have been in the lobby so openly unless they had a reason, and a reason could only be supplied by a master.

Brenda darted to the section of the gym devoted to weightlifting before pacing back to drop a metal bar from a barbell next to Lily. She hefted the bar and grimaced at the weight as her arm protested. Pivoting, she faced the fire escape door as Brenda took up her battle stance. The sound of the vamps climbing the final flight filtered through the heavy door. Two stakes appeared in Brenda's palms and she went completely still, a predator awaiting its prey.

Lily couldn't manage complete stillness as her arms trembled. She hadn't yet regained her strength, but she gripped the bar with both hands and hefted it up as best she could.

The door crashed open and two gangly vampires filled the doorway. Their gazes went immediately to where Lily kneeled. A bad move on their part, because they didn't notice Brenda until she'd already flung the stakes right into their chests. The vamps clawed at the weapons for half a second before falling. Brenda dragged them both into the gym and stuck her head into the stairwell. She listened for a moment before slamming the door shut to turn back to the bodies. She knelt over them to make sure they were truly dead. Giving each stake a final nudge, she stood back up.

Lily lowered the bar, the threat over for the moment and focused her attention on Sophie. Her little sister looked more tired than scared, trusting Brenda and Lily to keep her safe. Sophie took everything in stride, but when all you knew was running for your life how else would you take life-threatening situations? She had been only two when their parents were murdered by the vampires and Lily wasn't sure if she had more than vague memories of normal life. Lily wasn't so lucky. Her memories were crystal clear since she had just turned seventeen when they had barely escaped that night.

Cupping Sophie's ponytail, she let the silky strands run through her fingers. "How you doin', Soph?" Her sister leaned into her without saying anything. Lily focused on Brenda prowling about the room. "How many do you think will come?" She looked toward the elevator bank and wrapped her fingers more securely around the metal bar.

Brenda considered her question, but didn't stop her movements. "Depends on if they find our scent on the stairs and whether the master goes to our room alone. He might not want to risk controlling the others in your presence, but once he realizes our room's vacant, he might send them out to search for you. I don't think this pair told anyone they spotted us. They were hoping to have you to themselves."

"So, we don't know what we'll be facing." She frowned in worry. The vamps had chased them into a corner. "We should have tried to make a run for it through the lobby."

"That's what they were waiting for. We wouldn't have made it near the door."

"If a pack of them comes up here, we won't be any better off."

"We have a chance it could just be the master."

Lily raised an eyebrow in doubt. Fighting a master didn't seem like better odds to her. She tried to see the super large room through the vampire's eyes. Make a strategy to defend herself and Sophie. Every moment was one moment closer to them being found. She needed to be focused for the fight to come. A large bang echoed up the stairs and Brenda snatched Sophie out of her arms. Lily stood and hefted the metal bar up as she followed Brenda to the farthest wall away from the main entrance and back staircase. She took Sophie as Brenda pivoted to face the threat. Sophie wrapped her arms and legs solidly around Lily.

A single vampire emerged from the doorway. Evil radiated from him and his soulless eyes.

The master vampire.

Looking past the two dead vampires and Brenda's impressive battle stance, he focused on Lily. Death gleamed in his smile.

Her heart stuttered and she forced her eyes away from his face. She set Sophie down and kneeled beside her, keeping her mouth close to her sister's ear. "You need to run, sweetie. Can you run for me?"

Fear passed through Sophie's blue eyes for the first time. "You can't leave me."

"I'll be right behind you."

Brenda pulled out a cursed silver dagger with one hand and a wooden spike with her other, distracting the master away from the sisters as he focused on her movements.

Lily set Sophie apart from her and pointed to the stairs by the elevator. "I need you to go and hide. Remember the hiding games Brenda practiced with you. We're gonna play now."

Sophie made it to the entrance of the workout area before she turned and cast a fearful look toward the master as he moved in on Brenda.

Lily jerked her attention away from Sophie. Brenda and the master leapt at each other. The master far outmatched Brenda who had always amazed Lily with her swiftness and fighting ability. She stepped forward to back up Brenda, but hesitated not wanting to risk hitting Brenda with the pipe. She glanced back at Sophie, frozen beside a treadmill, her eyes wide in her petite face.

"Go!"

Sophie started to cry and shook her head in denial. Fear for her sister made Lily move closer to the snarling vampires. If Sophie wasn't going to get herself to safety, it would be up to her to keep her sister from a horrible death.

Brenda suddenly froze and fell. Disbelief and terror lanced through Lily. Brenda's dagger and stake were buried deep in her own chest. The master had used her own weapons against her. Sophie's scream filled the gym.

He smiled over Brenda's dead body and beckoned to Lily.

Everything Brenda had taught her flew right out of her head. Pure terror filled her as if she was drowning.

He stepped over Brenda's lifeless form, his gaze sliding past Lily to where Sophie continued to make small keening sounds. "She's a tasty morsel, but you're delectable. I'll save her for dessert."

The terror fled as the power within rose up at his words. She would protect her little sister. Her fingers trembled as she filled with a white light, the same light that made her a target to every master vampire and dark creature in the first place. Her hand heated and flashed to burning as she flung it toward Brenda. The dagger, buried deep in Brenda's chest, released and rose up to fly into the master vampire's back. The stake followed shortly behind it.

His smile froze as his body registered the impact and he reached back in vain to pull the weapons out. He pitched forward with a body shaking rattle.

Not believing what she'd done, she stood frozen for a full minute. Staring at her hand, the burning sensation faded away and she clenched it around the metal bar, hefting it up with both hands. She had to check on Brenda. Perhaps she wasn't dead, as she appeared to be. Lily stepped carefully around the master vampire.

Sophie broke her petrified stance and ran to her, making a wide berth around the dead vampire. Sophie grabbed on to her arm, but she couldn't focus on her distraught sister just yet. The power she couldn't control surged within her. She knelt beside Brenda and instinctively ran her hands over the wounds. Her fingers tingled and burned. White light shot out of her palms and into Brenda's body. She placed her hand over the worst wound on Brenda's heart, blood seeped up through her fingers.

A breath shuddered out of her protector's body. She jerked awake, her eyes snapped open and focused on Lily. "Where is he?"

"Dead," she whispered another type of exhaustion besides fatigue filling her. She reached out to Sophie, drawing her closer.

Brenda grimaced in pain as she rose up on her elbows to verify the threat was indeed taken out. Her eyes narrowed at the sight of the fallen vampire. "He's not the only vampire in the building." She flinched as she pushed herself up into a sitting position and examined her wounds. "What did you do?" She didn't sound too thrilled with Lily bringing her back from the dead.

"I don't know." Lily shook her head. "Now probably isn't the time to discuss it." Standing up, she helped Brenda to her feet. "Can you run? I have a feeling we're going to do a lot of running."

"I'm gonna have to." Brenda held her hand out for Lily's bar. She shot a regretful look at the cursed dagger buried deep in the master vampire.

Lily understood her regret, but they couldn't risk removing the dagger in case it was what was keeping the vampire down and not the stake. She scooped the now silent Sophie up and kissed her tear-streaked cheek. "We're getting out of here."

Brenda snagged the dropped duffle bag and her backpack before moving slowly toward the stairs they had come up and stuck her head in the stairwell, listening. With over thirty floors in the building there were plenty of places for the vamps to be waiting for them. She motioned for Lily to follow her and they went quickly down five flights before finding a floor that didn't stink of vampire. Brenda walked with obvious difficulty. Lily tried not to mull over the possibility of being attacked without Brenda able to defend them. Her power had fizzled down again after healing Brenda and she wasn't confident in her ability to call it up on command.

They walked swiftly down the twenty-fifth floor hallway to the elevator banks.

She melted back against the wall, Sophie secure in her arms. Brenda punched the down arrow and they waited for what seemed like an eternity before the arrow's light turned off and the doors swooshed silently open. Brenda had the bar ready for a pack of vampires, but the elevator was blessedly vacant.

"Let's go," Brenda said. Lily hurried to catch up with her, raising an eyebrow when Brenda hit the button for the second floor. "We don't need to announce our arrival. Especially..." She placed a hand over her chest and pushed as if to get rid of an ache.

"How hurt are you?" Lily whispered trying not to alarm Sophie.

"Enough that I think we should avoid a confrontation if at all possible."

Worry crawled up her belly at the vamp's admission to not having the strength to fight. "How do you suggest we get out of the building? It can't be long until one of them finds him."

"Housekeeping and room service are on the second floor. There's a service elevator that goes from there down to the main floor and garage."

"So, we head for the garage?"

Brenda didn't bother to nod as the elevator hopped and the doors opened. Their luck seemed to hold. There weren't any vamps in the hallway. Brenda stayed behind Lily out of cosmetic necessity. Thick wet blood coated the front of her chest. Too much to explain away if anyone happened to notice. Lily hid the streaks of blood she'd smeared across her own shirt with Sophie.

None of the kitchen staff paid any attention to them as they made their way through the kitchen to the service elevator. It amazed her how people could have supernatural beings all around them and no idea they could be five minutes away from their own death. She hit the elevator down key and listened as the elevator cranked up. The hotel obviously wasn't worried about keeping this one as silently running as the guest elevators.

She waited until the doors closed before she brought up her next worry. "What if they have someone waiting? He has sentries stationed at the other exits. He would have them in the parking garage."

Brenda nodded. "We have to exit at some point."

"The garage won't have many people."

"Our advantage."

"How? They can attack us without fear of anyone else stepping in."

"That's why they have so many in the public areas. They figure we'll try to stay with the crowds. Safety in numbers. They aren't expecting us to go where they would be more comfortable. What they're forgetting is I know they won't be able to restrain themselves once they get close to you. Public or private won't matter, they'll attack."

"You make it sound like I'm a giant neon light."

"Might as well be. You could never blend into the crowd with a vampire watching."

"We've never really tried."

"And we aren't going to try now." Brenda dropped the duffle below the elevator bank buttons. "Step back."

She nodded, shifting to the corner of the elevator with Sophie secure in her arms. The elevator door laboriously opened and Brenda stood ready for any vampires. She was out the door before it finished opening and made impact with someone. Several thuds and grunts echoed in the garage. The silence that followed was just as loud as the fight.

Brenda stuck her head back into the elevator and snagged the duffle. "Let's go!"

Lily shifted Sophie slightly and followed Brenda out. A lone vampire lay on the floor next to a car.

"This way, there's a fire exit I doubt it's guarded. They weren't expecting us."

"They?"

"The other ran up the stairs, no doubt to get reinforcements." Brenda hit the fire door.

They ran up a single flight of stairs to the back of the building into a dark alley squished between two huge buildings. Hardly any of the city's lights filtered down.

"Head over there." Brenda pointed deeper into the alley where it wrapped around the other building. "Stay off the main street."

"Where are you going?"

"They're gonna be right behind us. I have a stronger smell right now because of this." She gestured to her injury.

"Your blood's on me. Sophie too."

"It's dried. Don't worry they'll follow me." She motioned down the alley again. "Go, I'll meet you at the safety point in the morning."

Lily bit her lip in automatic doubt but nodded and turned to jog down the alley away from all the vampires including her guardian.

L ily walked down the quiet road toward the emergency lights flashing in the night. Sophie was almost asleep and a dead weight in her aching arms. If their lives didn't depend on continuing to move and putting distance between them and the vampires, she would have dropped several blocks back. She worried over coming across a band of roving vamps. The darkness surrounding them wasn't helping her nerves.

Revolving blue and red lights beckoned to her like a beacon. Several police cars were parked in front of a convenience store, their lights flashing, but no sirens blared. She didn't allow herself to hesitate as she approached on the sidewalk. Hopefully Brenda was successful in her mission, but she couldn't count on it and there could be a pack of vampires quickly closing in on her. She had to get out of the heart of the city and fast.

Lily needed help. Slowing her steps, she wondered if she should try to get assistance and how she would convince someone to help her. The vehicles in front of the gas station were all police cars. Several cops meandered casually around. Whatever had happened here was over and they were wrapping it up. Her eyes met with an officer as he came toward her.

Her gaze locked with his. An instant connection zapped through her body taking her by surprise and she froze. He wasn't a vamp or a pet, but this sense of familiarity worried her. Her brain told her to keep walking, but her body didn't obey and he reached her in a couple of short strides.

Dark brown eyes moved from holding her stare to sweeping Sophie with a quick look. "You okay?"

His deep voice caressed her spine and she shivered in the hot, humid air. "I need help," she said, surprising herself by her own truthfulness. The bond solidified between them. He would help her if she could convince him. "We have to get away from here."

"This way." His hand caught her elbow and he propelled her to the patrol car closest to them.

As he opened the passenger door, another officer jogged toward them from the other side of the gas station. A vampire's pet had spotted her. She wasn't surprised a cop was a pet, but she wondered at how quickly he'd recognized her. She could barely tell he was under the influence of a vampire from this distance. He shouldn't have been able to see who she was.

Her officer followed her glance and shoved her roughly into the seat. Slamming the door, he ran around to the driver's side. His door thudded shut and he shifted the car into gear. The tires squealed as he spun the wheel to shoot out onto the street.

She looked over her shoulder, watching the blinking lights fade away as the car swerved down a side street. The engine roared as they raced down the dark road.

"Are you injured?" he asked.

She pulled her gaze from the rear window trying to see if the pet followed them. Her attention riveted by his warm eyes again, eyes that seemed to know what she was thinking. "I'm fine." She jerked her gaze away to stare at the street in front of them.

"You're covered in blood." His voice was even but loaded with tension. She wasn't sure how she knew, but his normal voice was much slower and relaxed.

"It's not mine." She needed to reassure him so he wouldn't insist on taking her to a hospital or any other public place where she would be found.

"The girl's?"

She shook her head. "She's uninjured. Someone else's."

With the hotel and pet far behind them her fleeing instincts were backing off to allow her brain to start communicating with her. Her brain wasn't too happy with the situation she found herself in. He'd just loaded a woman covered in blood with a small child in his car without a single question. Normal people didn't do that. He'd gotten her out of there as if he'd known who and what she was running from.

Lily forced herself to look at him again determined to see why he'd helped them and when he glanced to meet her gaze she focused on his eyes. They were alive with no sign of any vampire influence. His lips quirked as if he knew what she was doing, and he focused back on the road before pulling off into the parking lot of a mega box store.

* * *

Reyes Vega waited for her to say something as he shifted the car into park. Besides asking for help she hadn't said much of anything. He turned to her, resting his arm across the steering wheel as he tried to see her through the blinding glow of her aura. He'd noticed her as bright as a beacon walking toward the convenience store, a white light witch, just like his mother. Revving down his senses he was able to see her blue eyes and suspicious frown.

He supposed she had a lot to be frowning about, including finding herself in a car with a man she knew next to nothing about. Her intent had been clear when she'd read his eyes to make sure he wasn't under the influence of a vampire.

He checked the rearview mirror again to make sure no one was coming in the entrance. She was being hunted just as his sister had been. He hadn't been there to protect his sister. But he could protect this woman and the child she held.

"Why did you help me?" Her voice was soft like the features in her face.

He couldn't stop staring at her eyes. Whether she would allow his help would depend on his answer. "My mother would never forgive me if I let another white light witch fall to the vamps."

Her eyes widened in shock. "You know what I am. But you're not a..."

"No." He shook his head. Regret cruised through his veins. He would always wonder if he could have saved his sister if he'd been born with real powers. "But I know one when I see one. My mother's one."

"Oh." She bit her lip.

The gesture had him focusing on her mouth and a completely inappropriate shot of desire went straight through his gut. She needed his help not his lust.

The radio squawked with a familiar call sign, his. His supervisor was finally asking for a status check. He hadn't cleared the convenience store robbery with his dispatch when he'd darted out of there. He swore mentally and tried to think of what to say to Tony Faber. He couldn't risk bringing her into the station. The pet who had spotted her at the robbery scene wasn't the only cop in his department under the influence of a supernatural creature. Tony wasn't one of them, but he didn't know what Officer Dave Method might have already said to his sergeant.

Disappearing with a patrol car wasn't even on the table. If he failed to answer his radio for much longer, dispatch would put a trace on the car.

He grabbed the mic. "JSO Z-two F-three, seventy-seven, fifty-three citizen assist, en route to Urgent Care on Atlantic." He set the mic down as dispatch acknowledged his traffic. Tony's voice acknowledged quickly and then asked for an update on another officer. Turning the speaker down so he could still hear, but the audio wouldn't talk over them, he looked back at her.

"I want to thank you for your assistance." She hesitated. "I'm afraid I'm going to ask for more."

He smiled slightly to reassure her. "You couldn't shake me if you tried."

She nodded and he suddenly realized he had no idea what her name was.

"What should I call you?"

Her hand ran down the child's blonde ponytail. Amazingly, the girl was in a deep sleep. Her lips parted as she breathed. "Lily, and this is my sister, Sophie."

"I'm Reyes Vega. What do you need?"

"A safe place to hide for the night free of pets and vamps." The little girl shifted in her arms. The family resemblance between the two was incredibly strong. If he had to guess, the young woman had probably looked identical to her sister at the same age.

His first thought was his condo, but then he realized his home would be the worst place considering Dave would easily be able to look up his address. It had to be someplace where there weren't any vampires who would be able to spot her.

The doors to the store swished open and he frowned at the couple walking out. The woman's colors in her aura were off enough to concern him. Lily followed his gaze as he shifted the car back into drive and drove away from the couple before the woman had a chance to look inside.

"What is it? Vampire?"

He hesitated but shook his head. "No but could be a pet. Bad swirls."

"Swirls?"

A pet would have to get a lot closer to Lily to be able to feel the power coming off her. How had Dave known what she was? He should have been too far away to recognize a white light witch by sight. Dave didn't have any abilities as far as he knew which made him wonder if her and the child's descriptions were being broadcasted through the underground.

* * *

The roads remained mostly empty as they drove away from the store. He still hadn't elaborated on his cryptic comment. She watched him tap his fingers on the steering wheel and waited for him to tell her he needed to get back to work and his life. Lily remained silent hoping to get as long a car ride as she could before she would have to hoof it again. She had no idea where she was so the first thing she had to do was figure out where they were. Looking out the window, her eyes blurred from exhaustion and she wasn't sure she would even remember the street names she was reading five minutes from now.

"I'm going to call my dispatch. Just be quiet so they don't hear you, okay?"

She looked back at him and nodded. What was he going to tell them?

He flipped his cell phone open and pressed in the number with one eye on the road. "Hey Amber, it's Vega. Can you clear me from the Urgent Care? Yeah, flag down. Listen, I haven't been feeling well all night. I think I've got the stomach flu. I'm gonna need to go ten-ten. Great. Thanks, Amber. Yeah, talk to you tomorrow. Have a good night." He disconnected the call and set the phone down next to him before glancing at her again. "It'll be a couple minutes before she logs me out so we'll have time to get to the station and get my truck before anyone knows."

"Where are we going?"

"The station's a few blocks away." The car roared as he pressed on the accelerator. "We'll take my truck and go down to the river to lay low."

She tried to remember what she knew about the river, but even though they had been hiding in Jacksonville for a couple of months she didn't know much about the area. Sophie shifted with a whine and Lily slipped her hand under the small pack to rub her back as she hummed to get her to relax again. Of course, she'd probably wake up when they switched cars, but it couldn't be helped. Sophie needed the oblivion of sleep to forget. The tires squeaked as he whipped the wheel and pulled in behind the sheriff sub-station.

He parked the sedan right next to a truck. "Here." He pulled a key from his pocket and passed it to her. "You two get in and I'll grab my stuff."

Lily swung her door open, breathing deeply before emerging from the safety of the vehicle. Sophie stirred only slightly to snuggle tighter into Lily's arms as she unlocked the grey truck's passenger door. She slid in and shut the door behind her. A bench seat ran in the back, but she didn't want to relinquish her sister so she kept her in her arms. Reyes opened the driver's side door and threw in a bunch of stuff onto the bench seat. He jumped in, plucked the key she held out, and started the truck. Despite its old age the engine roared to life with the purr of a well-maintained vehicle.

The clock on the dash told her it was two in the morning as he drove down the back street behind the station. Sleep threatened to envelop her as the adrenalin continued to fade. Somehow, she forced herself to stay semi-awake for the most part, but when the truck bounced a curb she was pretty sure she'd nodded off at some point. Darkness surrounded the building he parked in front of. A small neon sign flashed "vacancy" in the window.

She rubbed her eyes and tried to get her brain functioning again as she looked out the window. Small cabins surrounded the main building where they were parked. The place looked like one of those cabin motels that usually advertised weekly rentals on the outskirts of a large city.

"I'll go in." In the dark, he unbuttoned his uniform shirt and unfastened his bulletproof vest, tossing them onto the bench seat behind him. A few clicks and his heavy belt and gear followed though he shoved something into the back of his pants. "Stay where I can see you."

She frowned, but didn't protest. The catnap had cleared some of the fog she had been functioning in. Why was she following his lead without any protestation? She only followed Brenda without question when there were vamps hot on their heels. The rest of the time she drove Brenda nuts refusing to do as she was told. But here she was, no vamps hot on her heels, being led around like a little child with a man she'd met barely an hour ago. An armed man.

He grinned slightly and jumped out of the cab to walk into the dimly lit office. In less than five minutes, while she sat there debating the pros and cons of staying or running, he climbed back into the truck and drove to the last cabin.

"Alls good, let's go," Reyes said, climbing out of the truck.

Lily followed, Sophie secure in her arms, and stifled a yawn as he herded her into the cabin farthest from the road. He flicked on the lone light and she was relieved to see it looked clean. But it wasn't your typical hotel room. A lumpy couch, small dinette table and a TV dresser stand greeted them.

He gestured to the door in the corner. "Bedroom's separate."

She peeked in. A queen size bed took up almost all of the small space. Laying Sophie across the bed, she focused on the task of stripping the child out of her bloody clothes. She pulled a shirt out from Sophie's backpack and slipped it over Sophie's head. Tugging the covers back, she tucked in her still sleeping sister.

Reyes leaned against the door jamb his expression searching, but when he spoke his words didn't reflect what he must have been thinking. "Go ahead and clean up if you want, I'll keep an eye out."

She waited until he stepped back into the front room before shutting herself in the bathroom. Thinking better of shutting the door, she cracked it open, so she could hear her sister. She made quick work of stripping out of her clothes. She kicked all of them into the corner and turned the shower on needing to wash off what had soaked through her clothing.

The shower woke her out of her stupor. Now fully awake, she stepped out of the low tub and dried herself off before pulling on the single change of clothes she kept in her backpack. Even after towel drying herself, her black cotton t-shirt clung to her. The grubby clothes in the corner brought the entire evening's activities back in stark detail. With a resigned sigh, she reached into the bloody jeans pockets and pulled out her pocketknife, her latest fake ID, and the small wad of twenty-dollar bills, transferring them to one of the pockets in the cargo pants.

Steam followed her out of the bathroom and she peeked at Sophie to make sure she was still asleep. Lily tip-toed to the bed and smoothed the covers over her sleeping sister. She watched her a moment wishing her second wind, or perhaps her third wind, didn't have her wide awake.

Chapter 3

Stepping into the small living room, she hesitated at the sight of the man she barely knew standing in front of the single window, peering out into the darkness. She studied him in the dim light. He was at least half a foot taller than she, almost six feet, and lean with a hint of muscles outlined under his shirt. His gaze remained on the parking lot.

A dash of panic skittered up her spine at his intensity. "Is someone out there?"

He shook his head, turned to her and smiled reassuringly. "Just keeping watch. I think you're safe for now."

She stepped into the room, noting he had made a bed on the lumpy couch. "Bathroom's yours."

"I'm fine." His voice was rough and he turned back to look out the window. "You should sleep."

"I'm awake now." The reminder of sleep made her wish she could fall asleep. It would be ugly when this latest burst of energy drained out.

He looked back at her as he hit the switch to turn the lone

lamp off. The room went dark except for a faint glow from the walkway lights outside.

She chewed on her lip. "You could sleep."

"I'm on graves. Won't feel tired till morning."

The darkness added a layer of intimacy to his voice. She went to the window herself to look out and make sure all was really silent. Amping her power up, she peeked out and he chuckled.

"What?" She looked back at him.

"You're blinding me." He closed his eyes briefly before glancing back at her.

She cocked her head not understanding what he meant. "How?"

"Your white light, it goes neon whenever you run hot."

Crossing her arms, she faced him, pulling it back in. "Better?"

"Yeah, we'll have to work on that."

"You going to tell me how you can see my light when you aren't a vampire?"

"A little late to be asking me such a suspicious question." He raised an eyebrow and smiled. "I told you my mother is a white light witch."

"But you can actually see the light. Normal people don't see the light. What are you, Reyes?" Her intuition told her she could trust him, but she wouldn't be led around any longer without answers. She had to know what made him different.

His dark brown eyes stayed on hers, his lips still curved into an amused smile. "I read auras."

The swirls comment outside the store suddenly made sense. "That's how you knew the other officer was a pet when you looked at him." Her own instincts allowed her to sense when someone was a pet or a vampire if she was close enough, but she couldn't visually see the difference. "Like a sign?"

"I know. Not very studly. My sister got the real powers. I got something pretty useless."

"You see people for who they really are. I wouldn't call that useless."

He shrugged, his eyes straying away for a moment before catching her gaze again. "It might be helpful, but it isn't useful when the shit hits the fan."

Lily almost laughed, realizing he was envious of her *gift*. She'd spent the last two years on the run for her life because of what she was. "You helped me because of what you can see. Your gift. If you hadn't, I'd still be running down dark alleys dodging pets and vamps."

"I doubt that." He looked back out the window. "The next step is to get you out of town."

"Actually," she hesitated at his narrowed eyes, "I can't leave town yet."

"Any particular reason?"

"We left someone behind and I need to meet up with her in the morning."

"I'll take you there."

"It might be better if we went on our way without you. I've complicated your life enough."

He shook his head. "I stick with you. I get what you're saying, but you're stuck with me for now at least until we get you to safety."

"I'm never safe." The words would have depressed her if she allowed them to, but she always shoved the feelings down when they wanted to emerge.

He grinned. "I guess you're stuck with me for a very long time."

His smile did funny things to her insides as a tingle went down her spine and everything within her started to ache. Reyes' smile faded as he moved away from the wall to take the single step needed to close the distance between them. His hand raised and his fingers caressed down her cheek.

He sucked in his breath. "Fascinating."

She stared up into his eyes. "What?"

"It's like a rainbow."

"Should I tone it down?" She wasn't sure she would be able to. Her power seemed to be surging along the path his fingertips took down her cheek.

"No, it's beautiful." His head dipped closer. He hesitated a second before his lips captured hers.

Warmth spiraled from the pit of her stomach out through her body, surprising her with its intensity. More than her magic flowed through her veins. It took her a single stuttered breath to realize it was desire. Every nerve in her body went on instant alert.

His hands framed her face, his fingers caressing her cheeks as he drew back to look in her eyes. His lips hovered over hers. "Beautiful."

Her eyes locked with his, unable to pull away from the matching desire she could see building. She closed the inch gap between them to capture his lips again. She wanted the warmth his gaze promised. His tongue traced her lips and she opened her mouth to give him admittance. An ache formed between her legs. His tongue swept into her mouth and his hands moved away from her face.

Flicks of heat followed the trail of his fingers as he slid them down her arms to her waist. He pressed her tight against the length of his body. Her entire body tingled and the ache between her legs grew more intense. She closed her eyes to focus on the feeling.

His kiss seemed to go on forever yet was over too soon when he pulled back and rested his forehead against hers. "Sorry."

She opened her eyes and met his. "For what?"

"I shouldn't have kissed you." His hand came up to caress her cheek.

"Why not?" She narrowed her eyes and tried to pull her thoughts together to figure out why he was apologizing.

His eyebrows came together in a frown. "Because—"

She didn't give him the chance to continue his excuse. Going up on her toes and wrapping her arms around his neck, she pressed her lips against his. She didn't want him to stop kissing her. He didn't fight or resist as she feared, but took control of the kiss as he had before. His hands explored her body slowly. They squeezed and molded, pulling her impossibly closer. Her power flowed through her veins enhancing the pleasure his touch triggered. His lips left hers and worked down to lick and nibble on the hollow of her neck and shoulder.

She caught her breath as her entire body began to throb. Edging close to him, she rocked her hips to bring relief to the throbbing. It didn't help. She wrapped a leg around his and he hoisted it up higher, shifting his own hips so his erection pressed right where she needed. She rubbed against him, the ache increasing even more, almost giving her the relief she needed, but not quite.

"Damn," Reyes ground out, pushing her up against the wall and pulling her other leg up so she straddled him. His breath heaved as he surged against her. "Lily, I want you."

His words spiraled straight through her body and she moaned. All shyness and inhibition gone in the desire she could feel radiating from him which matched her own desire. "I want you too."

He dropped her legs and unbuttoned her pants. She should have been helping him with the issue with clothes being in the way, but she couldn't tear her gaze away from his face. Her hands moved over his shoulders, pressing and testing the strength which had held her pinned a moment ago. He pushed her cargos off her hips and they puddled to the floor.

"Step up," Reyes whispered, his lips capturing hers again.

The conscious part of her kicked free of the pants, but the rest of her focused on his lips and she pressed against him.

The kiss grew more passionate and his hands moved up her naked hips to grab the bottom of her shirt. Breaking the kiss, he pulled it over her head. She felt the loss of his lips immediately and wrapped her arms securely around his neck to prevent him from pulling away again.

His body pushed against hers making it obvious she'd missed him chucking his own pants completely. She slid her fingers under his shirt, wanting to feel his skin. He shuddered and claimed her lips, his tongue thrusting in as he lifted her up to pin her against the wall.

Her legs wound around his waist without a thought. His erection pressed against her. His hands lifted and shifted her slightly, allowing his erection to press where she ached. His breath came out in ragged gasps. His eyes held hers as he lowered her down onto him.

She whimpered quietly at the invasion. As much as she wanted him inside her, it had been so long it might as well have been her first time.

"Shh." Reyes kissed her cheek, his chest rising and falling with his labored breath.

Squirming, she took a shallow breath as the pain started to

subside and her body accepted him. He slowly lowered her until he was fully sheathed inside her.

He held her still, his lips moving across her cheek to reclaim her mouth. The tension inside her built and she rocked against him. Her movement was all his body needed. His hands held her legs around him as he pressed her into the wall before slowly withdrawing and thrusting forward again.

The orgasm hit her. He swallowed her cries with his kiss, holding her tight against him. He drove more forcefully into her several times. His tongue tangled with hers. His groan moved up his chest as he surged into her a final time.

His lips left hers and his ragged breathing sounded in her ear as he held her against the wall. Slowly his hands shifted her and he eased back, setting her down. But he didn't release her, his arms came around her to pull her into his embrace and his lips brushed against her forehead.

She sighed an odd feeling creeping its way into her chest. A wave of exhaustion crashed through her body distracting her from whatever she had been feeling.

* * *

Reyes held Lily as she fell into a deep slumber on the makeshift bed he'd made on the floor. Her light dimmed when she slept. The distinct pattern of her aura vibrated clearly without her power flaring. He caressed the length of her arm and looked toward the window.

Her pants were on the coffee table next to them. He frowned, thinking of the implications of her needing her clothes within arms reach. She was so used to being on the run. She'd fallen asleep quickly in his arms confirming his suspicions that she'd been functioning on sheer adrenaline. She must have been using her white light ability to keep going long past mortal capabilities.

Inhaling the citrusy smell from her shower earlier, he untangled himself, careful not to disturb her as he stood. He needed to sleep as well since they would be heading out in the morning. But he couldn't relax until he checked the window one last time. The parking lot contained the two cars it had before they'd come along with his truck on the side of their room.

He padded quietly to the bedroom and looked in on the small sleeping bundle. Her aura wasn't as bright as her sister's, but her colors swirled strongly. Satisfied she slept peacefully, he went back to the inviting, if incredibly uncomfortable, bed he'd made on the floor. The room was hot and stuffy. No air conditioner. The open window let in a slight breeze as well as any sounds to alert them if someone entered the parking lot.

He stepped into his boxers before stretching out next to Lily. She'd insisted on pulling on her own panties and a shirt before allowing herself to succumb to sleep, another sign she was ready to leave in a second's notice. He caressed her arm again before flopping onto his back. It was too hot to cuddle. The feel of her skin under his fingers would have to satisfy him for now.

It took him a lot longer to fall asleep than it had taken Lily. He would be lucky if he slept an hour before daybreak came.

Chapter 4

The light filtering in woke Lily from her short sleep. The unfamiliar weight of a man's arm weighed heavily across her waist. For a second a sliver of panic worked its way into her heart and then memories of the night filtered through her. The panic changed to a warm, but slightly embarrassed feeling. Her cheeks heated as she shifted to look at him. His arm tightened as he came awake instantly.

None of the confusion she'd felt waking up seemed to go through his eyes as they focused on her lips. His face filled her vision and he kissed her. Slowly and leisurely. His arm tightened to bring her fully against him.

Sophie let out a soft cry from the other room. Lily pulled away immediately and rolled to her feet. She was in the bedroom and scooping her sister up in a few seconds. Sophie cried into her, coming out of the nightmare.

"Shh," Lily soothed, pushing Sophie's sweaty hair off her forehead. "It's okay, baby, you're safe. Sissy has you and won't let anything happen to you."

Sophie whimpered, but opened her eyes to look up at her sister. She then looked around the room in confusion. Her gaze locked on Reyes standing in the open doorway. He smiled reassuringly. Lily found she couldn't draw her eyes away from him. She hadn't consciously realized how striking he was with his dark hair and eyes until this moment.

"Who's he?" Sophie whispered.

"He helped us last night, sweetie."

Sophie's forehead wrinkled as she frowned at him, but smoothed out after a moment as if remembering him. Lily hugged her until the tension eased from her body.

"I'm hungry," Sophie whispered into her ear.

"Me too. Let's get dressed and we'll find something to eat."

Reyes headed into the bathroom with a quick smile and wink. He shut the door and the shower turned on.

"Is he staying with us?" Sophie asked.

"For now." Her thoughts strayed to what she'd done in the night. She pushed the images aside and focused on her sister. "Let's get you dressed and then we can see about finding something to fill your tummy."

She tickled Sophie's stomach on the word tummy. Sophie laughed, throwing herself out of Lily's lap to the middle of the bed. Lily looked at the cheap watch on her wrist and frowned at the just after eight a.m. display. She couldn't believe she'd slept this late even with everything that had happened throughout the night. They'd be safer from any packs of vamps now, but Brenda would be worrying about them. Jumping up from the bed, she pulled out the extra change of clothes from her sister's backpack. It felt almost routine except for the addition of the man she had just met, but already slept with.

She didn't sleep with men she barely knew. Her previous

experience had been two boyfriends in high school before her world had come crashing down. Last night's encounter had been nothing like what she had previously experienced.

But why him? She didn't even know if she could trust him. He hadn't done anything overt to violate her trust except help someone he didn't know. Normal people didn't drop everything to help a complete stranger as he had. Just because she was drawn to him on a primal level didn't mean she should automatically trust him.

The shower turned off and she realized she'd been sitting there staring at the bathroom door as her doubts ran through her head. Sophie stood next to the bed watching her.

He stepped out, dressed in faded jeans and a blue shirt, and all her doubts fled at the sight of him. She could use any help he was willing to give. His lips were pulled down into a frown, but raised up as Sophie peered at him. "You ladies ready to eat?"

Lily scooped Sophie up and thought briefly of giving her a shower as well, but they needed to meet up with Brenda. Hygiene could wait until after. "One second."

He headed into the living area. Sophie jumped up and stepped into the leggings Lily held out for her. She strapped her sister's sneakers on her feet next and set her on the floor before following Reyes out into the room. The sight of her pants on the coffee table made her realize she'd completely forgotten to finish dressing herself.

Her cheeks heated as she hurriedly pulled them on and shoved her own feet into her sneakers. Reyes looked out the window and didn't appear to notice her discomfort.

He turned. "Where to?"

She took a deep breath as she looked into his eyes. They were the same. No evasiveness, just the desire to help. She made the leap to trust him once more. "The arboretum."

"Why are we going there?"

"My friend will be waiting for us."

His eyes narrowed on her, but flicked to Sophie for a moment. "We'll get something to eat first, then head to the arboretum."

She nodded, relieved he wasn't going to push her on who her friend was. She slung both her and her sister's backpack over her shoulder. He opened the door and they filed out of the room to walk the short distance to his truck. He tossed his bag on the bucket seat in the back and reached for Sophie. Lily hesitated at not having her sister in her arms.

"She'll be safe there." He pointed at the front dash. "Airbags."

Her sister rarely spoke in front of others beyond basic needs. She smoothed a hand over Sophie's tangled hair. Reyes raised an eyebrow and she nodded, passing Sophie gently off. He buckled her in the middle so she could see out between the two bucket seats. Smiling, he produced a small stuffed cat with a flourish.

Sophie hesitated a moment before allowing him to give her the toy. Reyes stepped out of the opening and gestured for her to climb in. Lily slid into the seat. She sucked her breath in when his hand moved to her arm and the familiar trail of fire followed the path of his touch. An answering flame reflected in his eyes. She held completely still as he buckled her in.

Pulling back, he whispered in her ear. "Just seeing if I was imagining it last night." His lips curved. "I wasn't."

He shut the door and moved around to the driver's seat to pull out of the parking lot.

* * *

A quick drive through a fast-food chain was all the breakfast Reyes allowed them. They'd finished eating by the time they reached the parking lot of the arboretum. Lily hesitated, looking around for any sign of danger.

"What now?" Reyes asked.

"We go in. She'll find us."

"Others could find you as well." His voice clearly showed he didn't like this idea.

"We can't leave her." She smiled at Sophie. "Right, sweetie?"

Sophie nodded solemnly; the cat clenched in her small hand. "Brenda protects us."

He started to say something, but instead climbed out of the truck. Lily followed suit and got Sophie out. They didn't have to wait in line to get in since it was still early. Picking the wildest trail she could find, they started walking. Sophie actually wanted to walk too. Lily let Sophie skip a few steps ahead of them as Reyes slowed her down with a hand on her arm.

"Who is she?" he whispered.

"Our protector," she answered in her own low voice.

The jungle quickly surrounded them and she tried to keep her ears alert to any out of place sounds.

"Where was she last night?"

"Leaving a trail for the vamps to follow so Soph and I could escape." She kept her gaze on her sister even though her body was focused completely on Reyes.

"They could—"

Something hard shoved Lily and she sprawled onto the dirt path. Sophie let out a small scream. On instinct, she scrambled forward to scoop her sister into her arms. Prepared to run for their lives, she spun to take in the new threat.

Chapter 4

* * *

Reyes stared into the burning eyes of a vamp. She had him pinned flat on his back, one hand wrapped around his throat.

"Wait. Stop," Lily said, her voice forceful and determined.

The vamp snarled in his face. "He smells of you."

"Yes, he helped us."

The vamp's eyes narrowed and she sniffed again before looking up disdainfully. "You mated with him."

Seeing her attention shift, he tried to flip her off, hoping her diverted attention would give him the chance he needed. But she didn't budge. He couldn't budge, his arms still effectively pinned by her knees and he was rewarded for his effort by a sharp pain lancing up his left arm.

He sucked in his breath and his vision blurred.

"Yes." Lily's voice was soft.

"Good thing or he would already be dead." One moment he was trapped and then in the next, the vamp was off him and several feet away.

"Reyes!" Lily dropped down on her knees next to him. Her hands glided gently over his arm as spots filled his vision. "You broke his arm!"

He breathed through his teeth. So, that explained the shooting pain. He needed to get up, but when he tried to move the pain seared his nerves. He closed his eyes against the spinning world.

Lily's hands were feather light and warm as they rested on him. The throbbing pain diminished until it was manageable. The warmth from her hands encircled him. He opened his eyes with a jerk. She was blinding with the shining light radiating from her.

The heat in his arm intensified. "Lily?"

"Shh," she whispered. "You're okay."

And he was. The throbbing vanished. Her hands left him and the glaring brightness suddenly flickered off. Lily swayed. Surprisingly, his arms moved to grab on to her shoulders.

"We should have just left him," the vamp said acidly, stepping closer.

Despite Lily's apparent weakness, she glared over his head to where the vamp stood. "Should I have not come back for you?"

"Come on, Soph," the vamp said, the little girl secure in her arms and a black bag slung across her back. "Enough talk. We have to move."

Lily sighed, but didn't appear to be alarmed by the sight of her sister being carried off by a vampire.

"You didn't mention your friend was a vampire." He sat up, trying to work his mind around the latest twist. Sophie's bright blond head contrasted against the vamp's long black hair.

"I hoped to introduce you first."

"But she attacked before you could."

"Brenda takes our safety very seriously. We should go," she hesitated, "or we can separate here."

He narrowed his eyes as he stood, flexing his arm – there was no sign it had recently been broken. It felt exactly the same. He focused back on Lily. He wouldn't leave her with a vampire. "You can't trust her."

She smiled. "Yes, I can. She's been with us for a year and has never even attempted to influence my light let alone take it."

"Why?" He had a hard time believing any vampire could exert that much self-control. He stared down the path as Sophie moved her hands around animatedly speaking to the vampire.

She bit her lip. "Come on." She started walking. "Let's just say not all vampires feel absorbing a witch's light is a good thing. But since you can't kill one without the light seeking somewhere else to go, they work on keeping us alive."

He didn't know if he believed her or even if she was telling him the entire story of what was between her and the vamp. He flexed his arm again as they rounded a bend where the vamp waited a few feet away.

Brenda's eyes were hidden behind large sunglasses. He supposed in concession to the sunlight they were about to step into. Being a vampire in the twenty-first century had its perks. Sunglasses, sunscreen, and SPF protected clothing allowed them to walk among the living, day or night, though few vampires could manage daylight and direct sunlight for an extended length of time.

The vamp's lips curved into a snarl. "You're the one whose motive should be questioned. I've been with Lily for over a year and you show up just when she needs help and have attached yourself to her in every possible way."

Sophie closed her eyes in response to the venom in the vamp's voice. He fought the urge to snatch the child from her. There was no way he could match the vamp for strength – he'd already learned that the hard way. It pissed him off even more when he could see Lily listening to what the vamp was saying. Her gaze was full of questions and unease.

So much for personal tragedies remaining private.

"My sister was killed by a vampire for her witch light," he ground out, staring straight at the vamp, mentioning his sister's death always made his heart clench in pain. "I'll be damned if I'll step aside to allow someone else to suffer the same fate when I can prevent it."

Lily touched his arm and he restrained himself from shrugging off her comforting touch. "I'm sorry."

"I don't like to talk about it." He didn't take his gaze off the vamp. "Obviously, it's a painful memory."

The vamp's lips curved into a humorless smile. "Obviously, it would generate the right amount of sympathy."

He wasn't surprised the vamp wasn't inclined to believe him. "Ask my mother, who's also a white light witch. She barely escaped the master when he attacked. My sister wasn't as lucky."

This time a considering look crossed the vampire's face. "Where's your mother?"

"Brenda?" Lily questioned.

"It's time to leave town anyway." The vampire set Sophie on the ground and took two measured steps toward him. "If you're serious about us being able to verify your story with your mother?"

"Do you really think I'd lead a vampire straight to my mother?"

Lily's grip increased and she stepped between him and the vampire. "Of course not." She rose up on her toes and pressed her lips to him.

Despite the nearness of the vampire, a spurt of lust shot straight to his groin at the contact.

"I would never ask you to risk your family or yourself. Thank you for your help, Reyes." She smiled sadly. "Maybe we'll meet again sometime."

A slash of panic made his stomach clench as she drew away and he gripped her arm this time. "Wait."

She shook her head, her smile gone. "You don't need another witch to take care of. Not to mention a child and a vampire"

He glared at the vamp. "I can't walk away. I don't want to walk away. We'll visit my mother if that's where you want to go."

"Reyes—"

"No." He scooped Sophie up who had come to stand next to him and began to walk. Thankfully, the little girl didn't object, but looked at him with a compassion way too old for a child so young. She touched his cheek with her small hand and a feeling of warmth seeped in. "We're burning daylight. It's a long drive."

He could hear the vamp and Lily following behind, but neither of them said anything.

Chapter 5

"You've never mated with a man as long as I've been with you." Brenda never bothered with small talk.

Lily glared at her. Reyes was close enough to hear. She pitched her voice lower. "It's none of your business."

"It is. The only reason he isn't dead is because you mated with him. How did you know I would hesitate to kill him with your smell on him?"

"I didn't." She frowned considering what the vamp said. She hadn't exactly been thinking when she'd been with him. "Look, he's helping, isn't he?"

Brenda was quiet for a moment. Her hand touched Lily's arm briefly "You don't know him."

"I didn't know you when you saved us."

Brenda had come into their lives the same way Reyes had. They had been under attack by a group of vampires and suddenly Brenda was there, but instead of attacking Lily she'd gone after the group of vampires. Her actions gave her and Sophie the chance they'd needed to run away. Brenda had caught up with them, explaining that not all vampires wanted to kill a witch for her powers. It had taken a lot longer for Lily to trust Brenda than Reyes.

But she'd known the instant she'd stared into his eyes that he would protect them. She still didn't understand the familiarity they shared, but her gut told her he was sincere in wanting to help them. Why else would he willingly accompany them with a vampire tagging along?

* * *

Reyes tried to keep his irritation and boiling emotions down so he could be aware of what was around them as they walked into the parking lot. No one's auras seemed off as far as he could tell, except for the vamp behind him, who didn't have one.

He unlocked the truck before turning back to Lily and the vamp, confident he had himself under control. He would help her. Just as he'd explained to the vampire, he couldn't allow another white light witch to suffer the same fate as his sister. As long as he could step between the danger and Lily, he would remain. But what he hadn't said was that he seriously feared a part of his willingness could be because he was falling in love with her.

He didn't believe in love at first sight. What he felt had to be lust and responsibility, not love.

Lily had a hesitant look on her face, but the vamp's expression was much more expectant.

"My mother lives in the Keys," he said by way of explanation. "It's a long drive."

The vamp frowned. "We could get trapped in the Keys."

"If they found you," Reyes said. "She's been there since my

sister was killed and hasn't had a single problem. She went there for a…healer who lives down there. My mother survived the attack, but was injured."

"Why didn't you stay with her if you're so set on making sure another witch doesn't die?" the vamp challenged, stepping right up to him.

"Enough, Brenda!" Lily put a restraining hand on the vamp's shoulder. "I told you, I sought his help. He's offered and I've accepted."

"He could be leading you to a trap," Brenda snarled.

Lily looked pointedly at Sophie in his arms. "Do you really think so?"

The vamp frowned at the little girl nestled in his arms. "Okay fine. I see your point."

But he didn't. He also wasn't going to ask right now. He would ask Lily when the vamp wasn't within biting distance. Lily smiled tentatively at him.

"Come on." He opened the passenger door.

Sophie climbed in and through the middle console to the back seat. The smallness of the cab hit him. Shit. The vamp would either be beside him or right behind him. Way too close for comfort.

"Brenda's been up all night." Lily stepped closer to him.

But her gait was off, hesitant. He didn't like her hesitating around him.

"I'm fine," the vamp insisted.

He jerked his head to the truck bed with its shell. "I've got some blankets we can lay out."

It would put some breathing distance between him and the vamp.

"Thank you," Lily said.

He narrowed his eyes as he walked to open the tail gate and gestured to the plastic bin in the back. "Blankets are in the bin."

The vamp gave him an icy smile and gracefully climbed up. He shut the tailgate with a resounding thunk and dropped the shell's door down. Lily climbed into the truck without another word. He walked back muttering to himself about irritating, blood-sucking vampires ruining everything. He closed his mouth as he slid into the cab and started the engine. A quick glance in the rearview mirror showed the vamp hidden out of sight.

Sophie smiled at him in the mirror and he smiled back without consciously realizing it.

"I know this is uncomfortable for you," Lily said.

He took his gaze from the mirror to Lily as he put the truck in drive and looked back to the road calculating how long it would take to get to his mother's house. "I wouldn't use the term uncomfortable."

"Terms are crucial around Sophie. She's heard and seen way too much as it is."

He glanced at her quickly before focusing on Sophie again who watched them expectantly. He took her warning and nodded to show he understood. "Uncomfortable works."

Her lips curved into an amused smile. "Brenda makes most people uneasy on her best days. She's very protective of us."

"I noticed." He flexed his arm amazed he couldn't feel a single sign it had been snapped less than an hour ago. He examined Lily, judging her complexion. She'd been running screaming hot to heal him and it had to be wearing on her. But you would never know by her calm demeanor. "Do you do a lot of healing?"

Her smile dropped a fraction. "No, not very often."

"You don't look drained." He cast another glance toward her.

"Is it easy for you?"

Her mouth opened and then she bit her lip as she looked down at her hands. "I wouldn't say it's easy. I don't know how I do it. You were hurt and the energy released into you."

He frowned and glanced in the mirror to collect his thoughts. The vamp was still out of sight. "It didn't make you tired?" When his mother had done something requiring as much energy as Lily had generated she'd always been exhausted for at least several hours after.

She shook her head as she pulled the band out of her hair and swept it back up into a ponytail. "Why? Should it?"

He didn't know enough about white light ability to answer her question. His only examples being his mother and younger sister who had just begun to grow into her powers when she was murdered. He shoved the thought aside. "From what I know, using your power is just like doing anything physically taxing. If you're just using a little you won't feel the effects, but if you get near your limit exhaustion can quickly overtake you."

Her hands moved restlessly before settling on her legs and she turned to him with a frown. "I don't know what my limit is."

"You're running hot right now." He was almost used to the brightness constantly surrounding her.

"Always. Does it bother you?"

He shook his head. "No. You don't run hot when you sleep."

She glanced over her shoulder at her sister. Sophie's lips moved though no sound came out as she played with her stuffed cat, having grown bored with the grown-up conversation. "I wouldn't know. It's...difficult for me to turn it off."

"You banked it down last night when I mentioned it." Like a dimmer switch, she'd seemed to turn it down.

"Not really, I sucked it in, but it never stops flowing." She bit her lip before speaking again. "I've only healed a few times when I had to. There's a touch of fatigue when I finish, but it's nothing I can't work through and it disappears quick enough."

He shot another careful look at her. She looked tired, but no more tired than when he first ran into her. Again, he wondered if she used her ability to keep moving when a normal person would have collapsed. Could be why she had to run hot all of the time. "My mom might be able to help you figure out how to control it if you want."

A small smile curved her lips. "I've never talked with another witch."

"I wish I knew enough about how it all worked, but I only saw them use their abilities occasionally and they didn't explain it to me when they did."

"Can you turn yours off?"

Her question took him by surprise. "Seeing auras?"

"Yes, can you turn it off like you're talking about turning mine off?"

"No, it's how I see. If I look at a person, it's just there." Should he be able to turn it off like a switch as he suggested to her? His mom and sister had rarely run as hot as Lily did.

"But your mother can?"

"I think so. From what I've seen she can." He smiled through his own confusion. No one had ever talked about his ability as if it was anything more than an oddity.

"I'd like to talk to her about it if she's willing." Her voice was quiet and contemplative.

He nodded, unsure of what else to say at this point, all of this talk about his mother was bringing up memories he would have preferred stayed buried, like the night he hadn't been there to save his sister or help his mom. He tightened his grip on the steering wheel until his fingers ached. His regret wouldn't bring her back and he breathed deeply until his hands loosened on their own.

* * *

The sea surrounded them, hemming them in with nowhere to escape. Lily took another deep breath to keep back the claustrophobia. Brenda had been right in her summation of this being the worst place to hide. There was nowhere to go if they were found.

Reyes hadn't said much once they finally hit the Keys. His face and body language screamed tension. She wondered if it was the memory of his sister or the upcoming meeting with his mother occupying his thoughts. The sounds of Brenda shifting around in the truck bed filtered through the open back window.

He turned off the main highway onto one of the many islands. She'd missed the sign so wasn't sure what island they were on. He obviously knew the roads as he expertly guided them away from the touristy areas to a stretch of smaller houses lining the beach.

The cottage he parked the truck in front of was small, but well cared for and cute with its bright blue colors. The street was quiet with only a few cars parked in driveways. He stared at the house a moment before sighing and getting out of the truck. She looked at Brenda to see if she'd caught Reyes' hesitation.

Brenda nodded. "I'll wait here. No need to frighten the old lady from the start."

Lily smiled before opening the passenger door and hopping to the ground with her sister safely in her arms. Sophie made it clear she had no desire to be held since being cooped up in the truck all day.

Her legs kicked. "Down."

"Stay with me." She set her on the pavement, but kept a firm grip on her hand.

Thankfully, Sophie didn't fight her, though her lips pouted a little as she looked toward the ocean. They could see a small strip of it between the houses.

Reyes knocked on the door and Lily walked quickly with Sophie skipping to catch up with him. She'd just stepped onto the porch when the door opened. The woman was beautiful. Soulful eyes and long ebony hair. Lily could see the resemblance between mother and son immediately. Just after the thought of how striking she was came the realization that she wasn't well. There was strain around her eyes and mouth.

Reyes frowned. "Mama?"

"Reyes." Her eyes widened as she looked past him to Lily. Did she recognize Lily as one of her own? "Who's this?"

He held out a hand and Lily took it tentatively. "I brought her to you. She was in trouble from…"

"Did you bring her trouble with her?"

"No." He shook his head. "Lily, this is my mother, Alandra."

Sophie ducked behind Lily.

"It's a pleasure to meet you." She summoned up her best company smile. The tension between Reyes and Alandra made it difficult to focus.

"Lily." Alandra's gaze flickered to Sophie. "And your daughter?"

"My sister, Sophie."

"She's not like you?" Alandra asked.

"No, not yet." She cocked her head. "How can you tell? My

light didn't emerge until I was much older."

Alandra smiled slightly. "And the vampire behind the truck?"

"She's with us," she said hastily.

"I assumed so since she got out behind you. Has she begun to drain your powers?"

"No. The opposite."

"She's her bodyguard," Reyes cut in. "Appears to belong to a group of vampires who don't believe any vampire should possess the abilities of a white light witch."

"And you believe her?" Alandra stared at her son in disbelief. "We'll see. Won't we?" She stepped back. "You're welcome to come in. The vampire is not."

Her words held steel in them. Lily cast a nervous glance over her shoulder to Brenda standing near the truck. With the vampire's acute hearing, she couldn't have missed what Alandra said. Brenda gave a tiny shrug and nodded, giving her okay for Lily to go in without her.

Chapter 6

Lily hesitated at the steps leading down to the beach. She'd come looking for him, but now that she'd found him, she wasn't sure what to do or say. Despite not knowing him for more than twenty-four hours his pain radiated in the center of her chest as if it was her own. She just didn't know what was causing the anguish. Selfishly, she hoped it wasn't her.

She walked gingerly down the old wooden stairs to the white sandy beach. The sun had already set and the moon glittered down on the ocean. Reyes stood where the waves rolled to meet the dry sand. The ocean was full of noise. It was noisier than she would have imagined. She'd always thought the ocean was supposed to be peaceful, but the constant sound of rushing and crashing water didn't relax her.

"You look worried." Reyes' words came softly across the sand. His eyes didn't leave the water and she wasn't sure how he knew she approached.

"Do I?"

He smiled as he turned to her. His happy expression didn't quite reach his eyes and the compulsion to apologize rose within her again. She forced it down. He wouldn't welcome another apology. The moonlight glittered on his eyes making them look darker and harder to read.

"What's bothering you?" His words were patient

She hesitated, looking at the waves. "You."

"And what have I done to earn your ire?"

"No ire." She almost smiled at his word choice. "You've been worried and that worries me."

"Broadcasting am I?" He glanced down at the sand and then back at her. "How much can you see?"

"Not much." She hurried to reassure him, wondering at the clipped note she could hear in his tone. "I can tell you're worried, but I think I would know without the extra stuff."

"Know me that well do you?"

His comment jabbed at her as she tried to figure out what he meant by it.

"Something's wrong with my mother." He started to glance over his shoulder to the house, but stopped the movement. "I don't know what. She never mentioned being ill."

It was obvious to her something was wrong with his mother's power, but she hadn't considered the cause being illness. "Her power seems muted."

He gave a jerky nod. "Yes, but it's more than that."

"She survived the attack from the vamps, but maybe the healer wasn't able to restore her."

"She was stronger when I left, hurt, but much stronger than she is now." He kicked the sand and she noticed he wasn't wearing shoes and his pants were rolled up. "Something's happened since then and she hasn't told me."

She realized with a sudden rush of clarity that what she felt was his anger at himself and worry toward his mother. He should have known something was wrong before now. Stepping next to him, she slid her fingers into his hand and squeezed. "What do you think's wrong?"

He shook his head, his thumb rubbing along the back of her hand. Shivers crept up her arm.

"She's ill. Her aura's dull and dingy." He took a deep breath as if steadying himself. "People who have auras like hers are usually…I think she's dying."

Her own mother's face flashed in her memory and her eyes prickled with the need to cry. She shoved the image out. He needed her support right now. Her own sorrows could wait until later. Much later if she had anything to do with it.

"But you don't know for sure that she is." She tried to reassure him. Something was wrong with Alandra, but it could be the lingering effects of barely surviving the vampires' attack. "I could see what's wrong."

His sharp gaze held hers. "What do you mean?"

She shrugged, not wanting to promise what she might not be able to deliver. "I healed you. If she's sick it could be something I could make better."

His face softened and he smiled for real. "I'd appreciate it." He raised her hand up to press his lips against her knuckles.

"I'm not promising." She wanted to make sure he understood she might not be able to do anything for his mother.

"I know," he whispered and tugged her a little closer to him. "Just look and tell me what's wrong. I won't ask for anything else. So, you can do that? See inside someone and see what's wrong?"

She bit her lip as her hip brushed his and she focused on his words not her body warming up. "Yes."

Unsure of how to explain how it worked, she opted to keep it simple and not explain that she didn't know how she did it. When she healed someone the answer was there along with what she needed to do to fix it.

"Where's Sophie?" His other hand went to her waist and he pulled her so she was facing him, her back to the ocean.

Her shoulders tensed at not being able to see the waves behind her and he automatically adjusted their position so their sides faced the ocean. "She wanted to see Brenda."

He glanced toward the road. "And where is Brenda?"

"Still hanging out in the back of your truck."

He grimaced. "Sorry."

"Don't be. It's understandable for your mother not to want a vampire in her home."

His gaze focused back on her face and she could see herself reflected in his eyes. "You're beautiful in the moon light."

His words were serious and her heart fluttered in reaction. "I thought I was blinding."

"Blindingly beautiful." His lips curved a fraction.

She narrowed her eyes and frowned. "Sarcasm isn't appreciated."

Laughing, he put his hands on her shoulders. "No sarcasm though…" His voice trailed off as he cocked his head. "You look," one hand moved up to touch her chin, "flipping young. How old are you?"

His silent perusal almost made her laugh and she raised an eyebrow in challenge. "How old do you think I am?"

"Young, too damn young." His hands ran up and down her arms, his touch eliciting a trail of fire. "You see, I have this unspoken rule. I don't date anyone who isn't old enough to legally have a drink with me."

She didn't drop her challenging expression. He couldn't be a day over thirty and she guessed he was younger than that. "You're one to talk, Grandpa."

He slid his fingers through her hair to cup her head and waited with an expectant look on his face.

The feel of his hands in her hair made her want to hum in delight, but she tried to focus on his question and what it would mean if he didn't like her answer. "Almost twenty."

He chuckled, his fingers moving in a gentle caress. His face dipped down and his lips hovered over hers. "Almost ten years, baby. Nearly a decade."

"But if I was two years older you wouldn't blink an eye about doing what with me," she whispered, tingling in anticipation of the kiss.

The corners of his lips turned up. "You do realize this feeling between us isn't normal. But then again, considering your lack of experience maybe you don't."

She narrowed her eyes in irritation. "I wasn't a virgin last night."

"No, but." His lips brushed teasingly against hers before pulling back far enough so she could see all of his face clearly. His fingers tightened in her hair. "You've been on the run for how long?"

She didn't want to focus on her life. She wanted him to kiss her like he had last night. She went up on her toes, sliding her hands up around his neck. But he resisted her tug.

"You didn't answer my question." His eyes were serious and the smile was gone from his mouth. "How old were you when they killed your parents?"

She tried to break the embrace, but he held on. She shoved

against his chest. "I don't want to talk about it."

"I didn't want to talk about my mother." He released his hold on her.

She frowned at him not wanting to admit he had a point. Hugging her arms around herself, she took a step back and considered. She often thought about the night her parents were slaughtered, but she didn't talk about it. Brenda had never even asked her.

"They came for me just after I turned seventeen. Something I did tipped them off to who I was."

"A vamp just had to see you," he said softly. "Nothing you did tipped them off."

She shrugged. She had always believed she'd drawn them to her. "I came home after a school dance. Didn't even realize my date was a vamp until it was too late. I think they were hoping I'd lead them back to a family of white light witches, but I'm the only one. I invited him in."

The cold gripped her and she couldn't speak. He brushed his hands against her and she jerked back. Closing her eyes, she tried to block the images out. The blood. There had been so much blood.

"My mother realized what was happening first. I never heard the pack come in until they were around us."

"I'm sorry, Lily." He kissed her cheek and pulled her forcefully into his arms. "It's okay, shh."

As he soothed her, she realized she was crying. He kissed her wet cheek again. A sob worked its way up her chest as the grief squeezed her heart. Shaking her head, she tried to force the feelings back to where they couldn't hurt.

His lips found hers and she clung to him, letting the pleasure drown out the pain.

"I'm sorry," he whispered again against her lips before trailing kisses down to her neck.

She opened her eyes. The moon wrapped them in its silvery embrace. The breeze off the ocean cooled the hot air surrounding them. Heat radiated from his body as he pressed against her. She combed her fingers through his hair as he nibbled and licked at her neck. Focusing on the here and now allowed her to pull back from the grief and only feel the sensations flowing through her body. His lips moved back up to hers, and she opened her mouth to let him in, rising up on her toes to press against him.

He groaned deep in his chest and broke the kiss. Resting his forehead against hers, he sucked in a breath. "We should go back to the house."

"Why?"

"Because if we keep doing this, I'm gonna push you down into the sand and have my way with you."

"Sounds promising."

He laughed and his hands moved back up to cup her face. "You're not running hot."

"I beg to differ." If she was any hotter for him, she would melt into the sand.

His fingers found their way back into her hair and his expression remained serious. "You're running dim is what I meant. You don't have to do that."

"Blinding you doesn't seem to be the best way to seduce you," she whispered, her gaze focusing on his lips.

"You came down here to seduce me?"

She shrugged. She'd come down to comfort him, to see why he was upset, seducing had actually been the last thing she was thinking about.

"You don't lie very well." His lips were gentle as he kissed her again.

Warmth spread on his gentle touch, surprising her with its intensity. She could feel his power increasing as he took his time tasting her. She tentatively let her own power flow slowly through her body. He chuckled before deepening the kiss. It switched from tender to fierce in a heartbeat.

They were wearing too much clothes. She wrestled his shirt out of his pants and slid her fingers along his hot skin. He broke the kiss again and dropped his hands to grab her wrists. Groaning in disappointment, she opened her eyes to glare at him.

His breath came faster, but his serious expression was in place again. "Let's go inside."

"Why?"

"This isn't a private beach and I don't think you'd enjoy getting sand in all types of uncomfortable places."

"There's no privacy in your house either."

"My mother's house." He leaned in for a quick kiss. "We'll just have to be quiet."

"Where?" From what she'd seen of the house there wasn't a "where" in it.

He considered a moment as he released her wrist and took her hand in his. "Bathroom?"

She laughed, picturing the tiny bathroom with its ocean theme. "Seriously?"

"We could explore some interesting positions." He tugged her back toward the stairs to his mother's house.

She flashed hot at his words. "Someone will notice."

"The couple walking their dog down the beach would surely notice us getting busy down here."

She glanced over her shoulder as they reached the stairs and sure enough she could see something moving toward them. Her first instinct was to run.

"You're safe." He squeezed her hand as if he felt her flight instinct kicking in. "No bad swirls, just an old married couple out for an evening stroll."

The adrenaline pushed the lust aside and she couldn't help the quick glances toward the couple as she walked up the wooden stairs to the back of his mother's house. She didn't stop watching them until he'd walked her into the kitchen and shut the door. A lamp glowed in the living room giving them a little light to see by.

Reyes frowned, touching her cheek lightly. "Relax. I'll go get Sophie and bring her back in for bed."

She started to nod and stopped, amazed at how natural it felt for him to be looking after her and Sophie. He didn't seem to notice her preoccupation as he stepped into the living room.

Chapter 7

Reyes stretched out on the chaise lounge and stared at the ceiling of the screened porch. Lily was in the living room with Sophie in the makeshift bed his mother had set up for them while he'd been kicked out here. Thankfully, it wasn't too cold or too hot, but it was too far away from Lily. He regretted calling a halt to their interlude on the beach. It didn't look like he would be getting a repeat anytime soon.

Thinking about last night made him hard all over again. He expelled a breath in frustration. It wasn't like she was leaving tomorrow or that he was some randy teenager, even if he felt like one, who only thought about sex.

"Reyes," Lily whispered through the screen in the kitchen.

It creaked softly as she came through. He turned his head to watch her walk toward him. The filtered moonlight glowed on her hair and enhanced her curves. Her long t-shirt barely covered her panties even with her gripping the edge to keep it down. She stopped at the foot of the chaise.

Her power dimmed down. He sat up and reached to draw her

against him. She moved willingly even eagerly into his embrace and snuggled on his lap. Not wanting to waste time, he pulled her close and found her lips with his. She sighed as she leaned into him.

Sliding his tongue into her mouth, he savored the taste of her. Her hands moved over his bare shoulders as she kissed him back, her tongue tangling with his.

He cupped her face with one hand while the other worked its way under her shirt to slide up her back. The softness of her skin enchanted him and he didn't think he would ever grow tired of the feel of her skin under his fingers. A quiet moan escaped her lips and he swallowed it, remembering the open door.

"Lily," he whispered, nibbling on her lips.

"Yes," she whispered back.

"I want you."

"I know." Her hands slid down his chest.

He closed his eyes to fully focus on the sensation of her touching him. "Just so we're on the same page."

She giggled and her hands dipped to his boxers. Desire shot through his veins and he reached for her hands before she grew too bold. She leaned in for a kiss and he obliged her. Shifting in the chaise to draw her closer, she moved to straddle him, surprising him into looking at her. Her power was banked down the lowest he'd seen it, but she still glowed like a beacon in the dim room.

She opened her eyes and smiled tentatively at his appraisal. "What?"

"You're beautiful." He moved his hand up to slide his finger down her cheek.

She leaned closer to him growing bolder. "You said that

before."

"It bears repeating."

She captured his lips and a moan worked its way up his chest. Squashing it down, he laid back pulling her with him.

"Reyes?" She snuggled against him, her arms going around his neck.

"Yes," he whispered against her neck as he licked his way to her collar

"This isn't normal, is it?"

He lost focus as he gripped her shirt. "What isn't?"

"The way I feel. I've never felt like this with anyone."

Satisfaction flowed through his blood and he couldn't help the smile curving his lips. "Me neither."

She leaned back and pulled her shirt off her head, revealing round perky breasts. She didn't try to cover them, but sat in his lap looking down at him. His erection nestled right where he wanted it. He would be inside her if it weren't for their clothing blocking her entrance. He was so intent on her breasts it took him a moment to realize she was waiting for him to say more.

"What do you want me to say, Lily?"

"I want you to reassure me we aren't acting crazy."

He focused his attention on her face trying to read what she was saying and why she would bring it up while sitting half naked on his lap. "If you don't want to have sex with me, say so."

Her lashes dropped, blocking her expression, and she leaned so her lips were an inch away from his. "I more than want to have sex with you."

"You can't doubt that I desire you since you're sitting on the evidence." He couldn't keep his confusion out of his tone.

Her lips brushed against his, enticing him all over again with barely a touch. "Then why aren't you taking me right now?"

He slid one hand down her back and wrapped the other one in her hair. "Because someone keeps asking me questions." He kept his eyes locked on hers and his hands in the safe areas. He was pretty sure she wasn't playing some sort of game with him, but something was bothering her about him…them. "I don't think we're being crazy."

Her lips brushed against his again and his entire body clenched at the sweetness of the kiss.

"But we are." She kissed him again and stretched out on top of him.

He wrapped his arm around her waist and rolled so she was pinned beneath him. Her lips curved and he sank into them, sliding his tongue along her teeth. She curled her arms around his neck to pull him close against her, her body arching underneath his. He was nestled just where he wanted to be and rocked once with a groan.

Remembering the protection he'd bought in the gas station on the drive down, he raised his face to look for his pants.

She frowned up at him. "Come here."

He smiled and kissed her sulky lips. "One moment." He reached down and pulled out the small box.

"Oh." A blush crept up her neck, striking him with her youngness again and he hesitated.

"Lily, we didn't use protection last night."

"I know." Her chin raised a tad.

He levered up on one arm so he could see her face better. "Are you on the pill?"

She shook her head.

He hadn't thought she would be and he fingered the box of condoms. "You could be pregnant."

She bit her lip. "I don't know."

"When will you know?" She shrugged and he narrowed his eyes wondering why she was being evasive. "You have to tell me."

She blushed again, but didn't drop his gaze. "It's irregular, okay?"

He nodded and registered her tense body below his. "Did I kill the mood?"

She slowly smiled and her embarrassment faded. "Utterly and completely." She touched his cheek with her fingers. "But I bet we can get it back again." Her eyes flickered away and then came back. "If that's what you want?"

Raising an eyebrow, he ripped a hole in the box with his teeth to pull out one of the condom wrappers. "I want."

She glowed happily and he tasted her lips, sliding his free hand over the curves of her breasts and down to her panties. He hooked his fingers in the waistband to slide them off and she reached down to help him.

"Reyes," she whispered against his mouth.

Her hands trailed back up to grab his own boxers and push. He quickly stripped them off so nothing lay between them. His eyes traveled the length of her body before he slid his free hand back up her inner thigh.

"Reyes," she moaned.

"Yes," he whispered.

"I need you inside me."

He groaned and captured her lips to kiss her deeply before pulling away. "I will be. Let's take our time."

She shook her head, her hand grabbing at the condom wrapper, her power flaring. "Now."

"Easy," he whispered, taking the wrapper away and opening

it to sheath himself.

He kissed her gently this time to help her tame down the flaring. She kissed him back, her hands sliding over his arm and back as she tried to tug him completely on top of her. He resisted, sliding his hand down between her legs to make sure she was ready for him. Slick heat met his probe and he closed his eyes for a moment before shifting so he was nestled between her legs.

Her hips rose beneath him and he braced himself on his elbows above her. His eyes locked with hers as he slowly slid into her. Her lips curved in happiness and he groaned, her power wrapping around him. He stopped once he was inside her and lowered his head to kiss her lips.

She met his kiss, her legs moving to wrap around his waist pulling him even deeper inside. "Reyes."

He closed his eyes trying to get a grip on the pure pleasure racing through his bloodstream. If he wasn't careful, he was going to embarrass himself in less than thirty seconds. He should have made sure she came before he entered her. "Yes?"

She sighed, her hands sliding up his shoulders to trail through his hair. Streaks of fire followed where she touched and he gritted his teeth against the pleasure. He grabbed her wrists and pinned them down next to her head as he surged into her. He locked gazes with her, stopping again.

He trailed his lips across hers unable to stop himself. "Don't move."

Her eyelids dropped as another sigh moved through her consuming him. "I'll try."

He nearly laughed at the absurdity of it, but focused on keeping control of the pleasure as he withdrew and slid into her. Her eyes locked on his, he could see her struggling to stay still beneath him, her lips parted again on another stroke.

She closed her eyes, her back arching as her body clenched around him, the climax hitting her. He quickly covered her mouth with his; surprised her orgasm came so quickly and rippled around him. He held back his moan as he pumped into her unable to hold back on his own release. He gripped her wrists tighter and surged into her warm languid body a final time, the pleasure ripping through him as he came.

He swore in his head at the intensity, burying his head into the chaise's pillow and her hair, unable to catch his breath. His lungs burned and his body collapsed on top on her.

Chapter 8

Lily stirred and opened her eyes. Dawn was creeping along the ocean. Night was no longer black, but fading into grey. She was squashed. Reyes' arm and leg held her down. She shifted to look at him, not that she could shift far. He lay on his side, giving her most of the chaise while he was pinned against one of the arms. She'd fallen asleep shortly after they'd made love, drowsy while he'd cleaned up before stretching out next to her again to sleep.

She looked at his dark lashes, strong nose, and stubborn chin. She wanted to kiss his perfect lips, but couldn't move. She sucked in her breath becoming aware of another presence. Moving her eyes, she kept her face still as she took in the shadow on the other side of the door. Reyes' mother watched them for a moment before moving back inside the house.

Crap! Of course, it had been his mother checking on them. And then suddenly she realized Brenda was also watching them, turning her head she glared at the outside screened door. The vamp's soft laugh faded off, but it was enough for Reyes to jerk awake. His gaze locked with hers. Unaware they had just been spied on by two people, he leaned in for a kiss. She held still for the moment, but she was unable to get the idea out of her head of his mother watching and couldn't relax.

"What's wrong?" he whispered.

"Your mother's awake."

He jerked, looking over his shoulder. "How do you know?"

"She was watching us a moment ago."

His eyes came back to hers. "Well, she's not now."

Lily raised an eyebrow in humor, but shook her head at his hopeful look. He sighed and sat up effectively freeing her from his limbs. She watched him as he unfolded and stretched in front of her. While she'd slid back into her shirt and panties before she was able to fall asleep, he'd left his clothes off. If they hadn't been spied on by two different people, she wouldn't have turned him down and right now she was a tiny bit regretting being responsible, but she scooted off the chaise and smiled at Reyes' wink before going inside to check on Sophie. And face his mother.

The house was silent and Sophie was still curled up in a ball. She grabbed her cargo pants from where she had left them folded by her pillow and pulled them on. Kneeling down next to Sophie, she brushed her sister's hair off her cheek. She smiled at the relaxed face and tucked her in while trying not to disturb the sleep that would end soon.

The pipes groaned and a shower turned on in the bathroom down the hall. She looked toward the bathroom and single bedroom relieved that she wouldn't have to face Alandra just yet. The kitchen screen closed softly and Reyes' feet padded in. He squatted next to her, his hand resting on her back. She glanced over her shoulder to see he was dressed, but his hair was still mussed and had the just woke up look to it.

"I'll make breakfast." He started to rise and looked toward the front door as if a thought just occurred to him. "When was the last time she ate?"

She shrugged, knowing who the she was. "She doesn't eat in front of us."

He frowned. "I sincerely hope she didn't kill anyone last night."

She was about to object, but something held her back. She honestly didn't know who or what Brenda ate. She'd preferred not to think about it since their protector never attempted to feed off them.

His gaze drifted back to hers, his face serious, but his lips kicked up and he kissed her on the lips for a second before going into the kitchen. The shower turned off and Lily hunched her shoulders. Almost as if sensing her sister's unease, Sophie stirred and opened her eyes drowsily.

"Hey, sweetie," Lily crooned, kissing her sister's cheek. "Good morning."

Sophie pouted and reached her arms up for Lily to scoop her up. Lily rubbed her back as she rocked back to stand and carry her sister into the kitchen. Reyes had his head stuck in the fridge.

He came out with a container of cut tropical fruit and a frown. "She's only got chick food."

She laughed in surprise as she sat at the small table by the window and cuddled her sleepy sister in her lap. "Well, since we're chicks I suppose it'll be perfect for us."

His mother entered at that moment, her long wet hair hanging loosely down her back.

Reyes set the fruit on the table and forced a smiled. "Morning

Mom. You got any real food?"

Lily looked down at her sister away from the tension between the two and had to wonder why Reyes would ask such an antagonistic question.

Alandra shrugged as she went to fill the kettle and set it on the stove. "I wasn't expecting you."

"Right." He awkwardly hugged his mother. "I can run to the store and get some stuff; do you need anything?"

"Actually." Alandra's gaze focused on Lily and she struggled to return the look. "I think it would be best if your friend and I started early. I get tired easily now and mornings are my best time."

Reyes frowned, shooting a concerned look at Lily. "Are you sick?"

She turned to her son. "No, why do you ask?"

"Your colors are…" He faded off at her dismissive look.

"I'm old. Not unwell."

Lily interrupted their awkward exchange. "I'm ready whenever you are." She smiled at Reyes to reassure him. She would see what she could find out about his mother's condition.

Alandra nodded. "Good. We'll need privacy and quiet. Perhaps, you could take the little one and the…other one to the pier, Reyes."

* * *

Lily kissed Sophie on her cheek and ran her hand through her soft ponytail in habit. "You're gonna have fun."

Sophie pursed her lips, looked to Reyes and Brenda waiting by the truck. Both were on the passenger side, but stood several feet apart. Brenda was in her day wear of hat, sunglasses, and long sleeves. "Why aren't you coming with us?"

"Alandra is going to teach me how to do some cool things, but she said we need privacy to concentrate. The pier sounds fun. You can play on the beach—"

"She has a beach here."

"Get some ice cream, play some games…" Lily bit her lip trying to think of something her sister would like.

"Will Reyes get me a friend for Taffy?" The stuffed cat was now her constant companion.

She smiled at her sister in relief. "I bet if you asked nicely, he'll get you whatever toy you want."

"Alright." Sophie nodded her head and released her iron grip on Lily's shirt. Even though she'd decided to go, she dragged her feet down the few steps to Reyes' truck.

He crouched down and whispered something in her ear. Lily rubbed her hands on her pants, the nerves suddenly hitting her at the prospect of Sophie being away from her. She rarely separated from her sister and had insisted Brenda go with them to keep her safe. Besides, Alandra wouldn't let Brenda in the house, so there was no point in her hanging out in the bushes hiding from the neighbors for a couple of hours.

Reyes scooped Sophie up and buckled her into the back seat. He didn't hide his grimace as Brenda climbed into the passenger seat. Lily bit her lip to keep from calling them back as they drove down the road. Dark grey clouds hung heavily in the sky where they were driving. A gust of wind suddenly hit her carrying the scent of fresh rain. Why hadn't she noticed the weather was turning?

"Ready?" Alandra called from inside the house.

Lily sighed and turned when she could no longer see the truck. The rain concerned her. Hopefully, there was cover on this pier

Reyes was taking her sister to. Worry gnawed in her gut. She wasn't clear why Alandra felt they had to be alone to teach her how to hide her light. She wouldn't be alone when she'd need to do it in real life.

"I've made tea." Alandra already sat on the small couch and poured the tea into green mugs.

Steam wafted up as Lily perched on the edge of the chair across from the couch. "How do we start?"

Alandra smiled. "I need to have an idea of your full range." She set a clear crystal on the table in front of Lily. "Can you make it glow?"

Looking at the rock, she wondered at the odd request. She'd never attempted anything like that. She only used her powers when necessary, not to play. Hoping Alandra had a good reason for the request, she focused her attention on the crystal and concentrated on amping her power up. The crystal vibrated for a moment, but didn't actually ignite as Alandra had suggested.

"Hmm," Alandra hummed deep in her throat.

Lily frowned, narrowing her eyes as she tried to make the crystal glow. It vibrated more violently, but still didn't light up. A small fissure in the crystal worked its way up her spine and she broke the connection.

Alandra tapped her finger on her lip before taking a sip of her tea. "Drink, it'll calm you. You have too much on your mind."

"Why didn't the crystal glow?"

"You were thinking of other things. You must clear your mind for it to ignite. Drink your tea."

She did as suggested and sipped the bitter tea. She wasn't quite able to hide the grimace and Alandra laughed.

"We don't always like what we need."

Taking another sip of the warm herbs, she was able to mask

her grimace this time.

"Good." Alandra nodded. "Do you feel the effects? It should calm and center you."

She didn't know if it was centering her, but she was certainly feeling calmer and sleepier. Thoughts of her sister drifted to the back of her mind. She stifled a yawn and took another bracing sip of the tea before setting the cup down hoping that would be enough to satisfy Alandra.

"Now, focus on the crystal. Give it everything you have."

Lily stared at the colorless rock and narrowed her eyes as she tried to draw her power within her. But it didn't respond. The crystal wavered and she blinked to clear her eyes. The crystal blurred and she rubbed her eyes, exhaustion overtaking her. Something was wrong. The world tilted and went dark.

* * *

Spending a nice sunny day on the boardwalk with a vampire was not Reyes' idea of a good time. Being stuck inside an obnoxiously loud arcade because the sunny morning had suddenly turned into a stormy, rainy day was downright unpleasant. He faked a smile as he paid for the ice cream he'd bought Sophie from the concession counter and handed it down to her. She took the cone in both hands and they walked to where a few small tables sat near the door. The rain pelted at the glass doors.

His edginess wasn't coming just from the vampire who ignored him as if he didn't exist, he'd also spotted several people whose auras were too damn similar to his mother's to be a coincidence.

He looked at the hamburger flipper behind the concession

counter and tried to make sense of the pattern and colors. The problem was he couldn't make sense of them.

"What are you glaring at?" Brenda asked behind him.

He jerked, not having realized how close she was and shifted his glare to her. "I'm not glaring at anything."

She looked to the counter. "You've gotten progressively jumpier since we got here and he hasn't done anything to warrant your appraisal." She sniffed. "Has he?"

He shook his head. "No." He pushed the similar auras out of his mind. He'd find out soon enough what was wrong with his mother. "What do you want to do next, Soph?"

She stopped mid-lick and whispered, "Sissy."

Her eyes grew large before rolling back in her head. He lunged forward and grabbed her before she hit the ground.

* * *

Lily jerked awake. Pain seared through her head making her want to scream. The last two years of being on the run helped her force the scream down and open her eyes. She was in Alandra's living room. Something bound her hands to the chair she was sitting in, but she could move her feet.

"She's awake." Alandra's voice came from behind her.

"You didn't give her enough." A new deep feminine voice responded.

"She passed out before she drank it all." Alandra's voice quivered slightly.

Lily turned her head, despite the pain, to look at the two women standing on the other side of the room. The light was muted and the rain drummed steadily on the roof. Alandra's hands twisted and her gaze was on the taller woman who was preparing something on the sideboard against the wall. Her hands moved quickly and efficiently. She didn't bother to look at Lily.

Lily looked down to her hands and the white rope that effectively strapped her into the high-backed chair she vaguely remembered seeing in the corner earlier. It now sat in the middle of the living room with her in it. She jerked her gaze back to the other woman. Not a vampire. A witch like her, but not quite. She fought down the unnatural fatigue pulling on her. The bitter tea. Alandra had put something in the tea or the tea itself had been the drug.

"What's going on?"

Alandra trembled. "You must do it quickly."

The other witch lashed out, smacking Alandra across the face. "You don't tell me what to do."

Alandra stepped back, her hand covering her red cheek and she nodded. "I'm sorry. I didn't mean…"

The witch smiled and crooned lightly. "It's all right. Come here." She put an arm around Alandra and gave her a quick hug. "You'll feel better soon."

"Yes, I haven't been feeling well."

"I know." The witch went back to doing whatever it was she was doing on the table.

Lily twisted her wrists trying to find some give in the ropes. She closed her eyes letting her power flow. She couldn't always control it, but it never failed her when she needed it desperately.

"There we go." The witch's voice was suddenly in front of her and she jerked her eyes open in surprise. "Let it go my dear."

"What do you want?" Her eyes locked on the small ceramic bowl held in front of her.

The witch laughed. "Your power of course. She tells me you

cracked the crystal. Remarkable really. Alandra wasn't even that powerful before I took her light."

She snapped her gaze to Alandra who fidgeted against the wall. She didn't understand exactly what was going on, but now she knew why his mother's aura was messed up and her light was barely distinguishable.

"Just think. No more vampires hunting you down any longer. You'll be able to live a normal life. Isn't that what you want," the witch crooned.

Her power flowed through her veins as her instinct for survival took over. She might not know what the witch planned, but she was in danger and had to protect herself.

The witch held the bowl to her lips and drank whatever she had concocted. She let the bowl drop and held her hands out in front of Lily's face. They began to glow.

Lily's power surged, racing toward the glow. She closed her eyes and shook her head trying to regain control. Her power wasn't trying to fight the glow, but was rushing for it. Pain streaked up her face as the witch touched her hands to Lily's forehead.

Lily screamed.

Chapter 9

"What the hell is going on?" Reyes ran behind Brenda through the pouring rain to his truck.

Brenda opened the door and buckled Sophie in. Against his instincts, he grabbed the vamp's wrist before she could climb into the driver's seat. The rainwater had already soaked his clothes and the vamps.

Her eyes narrowed a fraction. "Lily's in trouble."

"How do you know?" He dropped her wrist in panic.

Brenda gestured to Sophie. "She has her own powers."

He jerked a glance at the little girl who was beginning to glow faintly. The vamp hissed as she noticed the glowing.

"We're wasting time." She slid over, allowing him to get behind the wheel.

He started the truck and wrenched it through the packed parking lot before heading down the back street at double the speed limit. The wipers were on full blast and barely kept the windshield clear. "I hope you're wrong."

The vamp flashed her teeth. "Something we agree on."

It took nearly two minutes for him to finally reach the road to his mother's house. The truck soon screeched to a halt in front of the house and twin shadows emerged from the trees beside his mother's door. Vampires.

Shit! He opened his door about to run forward as Brenda was already leaping over the hood of the truck when Sophie made a noise. He looked at her realizing he couldn't rush in to save the day. She would be left alone and unable to defend herself.

Brenda faced off with one of the vampires. The other vampire had passed her and was walking steadily toward his truck. Her gaze locked on him through the downpour. He swore again in his head and slammed the door shut. Shifting the truck into reverse, he took Sophie away from the immediate danger.

The vampire leapt into a run as he backed away from the house. He swallowed another swear, not wanting to frighten the now awake Sophie, and pressed harder on the accelerator. He kept one eye on his mirrors to make sure he didn't hit anyone while keeping the other on the vampire in front of him. It was a female, but he wasn't stupid enough to think he could take her in a physical confrontation after his experience with Brenda. The little blonde was smaller than Brenda, but he couldn't chance it with Sophie. The vamp slowed as if deciding the chase wasn't worth it. He couldn't see Brenda any longer and he wondered what she was facing with Lily.

He might not be able to fight, but he could at least distract one of the enemy away. It would be a balancing act. Keep Sophie safe while tempting the vamp to chase them. He glanced quickly at Sophie before letting up on the accelerator. She didn't say anything and the light glow remained. Her eyes were closed, but he was sure she wasn't sleeping.

"We're gonna be fine, Soph," he found himself saying, worried about her lack of response to what was going on. Of course, maybe it was better she wasn't responding. With her eyes closed she couldn't see anything that would frighten her.

He focused back on the vamp before stomping on the brake. The tires slid before gaining traction and the truck jerked to a stop. The vamp's stride quickened as her interest in capturing them renewed. Slowly pressing on the accelerator, the truck backed down the empty street again. He just had to stay far enough in front of her to keep Sophie safe.

* * *

The pain subsided. Lily took another deep breath, fighting to center herself as she shoved her power down and away. It fought her, but it slowly receded and the pain lessened.

"No," the witch whispered. "Stop it!"

She found her center and pulled the light even farther within her. She would not let the witch gain power over her. The little she had seen between Alandra and the witch convinced her it would be very dangerous to allow the witch a spark of her light. The witch might not be threatening death as a vampire would, but she was trying to steal her power all the same.

The sounds of the room faded to an eerie echo and the witch screamed again, but not at Lily. At least she didn't think it was at her.

"She's useless now!" a voice shouted, but from far away. It sounded familiar yet not.

Something hit flesh and a body fell to the floor. Alandra screamed and sobbed.

Lily struggled to emerge from her trance, but her power started to spike and she renewed the effort to squash her light down. Her fingers tingled letting her know she had to open her eyes and find out what was going on.

Something heavy hit her and the world tipped before the chair slammed to the ground and slid several feet. Her eyes jerked open and she gritted her teeth to keep her power from surging as she tried to figure out what was going on around her.

"You will not take me!" the witch screamed.

Her wrist moved. The arm of the chair had broken from the impact. She wiggled it, pulling the ropes off, keeping her head still and trying not to turn her head to see what was happening behind her. She suspected playing possum was crucial at the moment. Her arm was free. She flexed her fingers and slid the rope across her stomach, tilting her head just a fraction so she could see the witch chanting and the master vampire smiling in front of her.

The coat the vampire wore was way too familiar as was the back of his head. He wasn't looking at Lily and the witch was completely focused on her own defense as her power amped up and surged. Several objects flung off the walls to bang into the vampire, but he barely moved.

A chill went through her as she slowly moved her hand toward the rope binding her wrist. It couldn't be the master vampire she had killed two days ago. Could it?

She worked the knot taking her eyes briefly off the pair to focus on what to tug on. The vampire suddenly lunged forward with blinding speed and seized the witch before she could raise her arms to protect herself. The witch screamed again and something heavy hit his back.

It didn't stop him. Lily flinched as the witch's scream turned into a high pitched squeal before fading off. Her rope loosened and she yanked her wrist from the confinement. She angled her head again, her gaze briefly sighting her belongings just a foot away in her backpack before focusing on the struggling witch and vampire.

The witch was limp in his arms as he fed from her neck. An odd glow surrounded the pair and Lily lurched to her knees to grab the pack, her searching fingers immediately grasping a long stake. She pulled it out and scooted around to face them. She wasn't sure where Alandra was, but the witch had stopped making noises and the vampire was completely engrossed in his kill.

She would have to move right now before he finished if she hoped to escape. Rocking back on her toes, she leapt up and ran four steps to the pair. The vampire raised his head just as she reached him. She refused to scream and put everything she had into plunging the stake into his back.

The stake buried deep into his back. Her hands trembled as they continued to move forward pushing it through his body into his heart. He spun, his hand going around her neck, but he was too late, and his grip barely squeezed before he wheezed and dropped to the ground. The light surrounded all of them, burning her as it released from the vampire's body.

She grabbed her head as her body flashed scalding hot as the light releasing from the vampire rushed into her. She crumpled down to her knees with a moan. A breath shuddered through her lungs as she tried to fight her way through the light. Closing her eyes against the blinding flash, the burning crawled over every cell in her body. She couldn't pull her power in or release it. She had lost control. Everything went dark.

* * *

Reyes wrenched the wheel of the truck at Sophie's cry. He jerked a glance at her and she appeared to be unconscious again, held up by the seatbelt. Swearing under his breath, he brought the truck full circle around the block and back down his mother's road. He was still in reverse which had earned him a few odd stares from passing cars on the busier crossroad. But the rain seemed to keep everyone else inside and no one seemed to notice the tiny vamp pursuing him. She was getting pissed now and he was going way over the speed limit in reverse.

A blur stepped into the road behind him and he stomped on the brakes. His truck slid to a stop an inch from Brenda. She leaped and thudded on the roof of the camper shell before jumping for the vampire in front of him. The little vampire, taken by surprise, didn't last long against Brenda's expert hand.

He almost jumped out again, but hesitated. Brenda didn't pause before pivoting and dragging the limp vampire back toward the house. He swore again, checking his mirrors. No one on the streets and he hoped no one was at their windows. Thunder rumbled. It was possible the storm was masking everything. He glanced at his mother's house. He didn't see any other vampires besides Brenda, who went in the front door, making him wonder why she hadn't already gone in. It had taken him a couple of minutes to drive around the block.

His mother stumbled out the door and he was out of the truck. Sophie made a protesting sound behind him and he hesitated, gritting his teeth as Alandra stumbled down the front steps. Brenda came out next carrying Lily in her arms. He looked around the neighborhood again before jumping back into the truck to drive over the curb and into his mother's precious flower beds. He braked just as Brenda reached them.

Sophie undid her seatbelt and climbed into the front seat in her haste to get to her sister.

"Wait," he said, but she was already scrambling out the passenger door and would now be as wet as the rest of them.

He jumped out of the driver's seat and looked around the quiet neighborhood. He supposed they were lucky the storm had hit. There wasn't a single person coming out to see why he was parked in the yard, but now the rain was slowly turning to a drizzle. People might be venturing out shortly.

"Is she alright?" Reyes asked Brenda, his eyes passing over Lily to his mother who hadn't moved from the shelter of her front porch steps.

Brenda sat Lily in the passenger seat of the truck. Sophie leaned in tight against her unconscious sister. At least, he hoped she was unconscious. Her light flickered and flared as if it couldn't find its pattern. Brenda nodded and scanned the area.

"What?" He looked around to spot what she'd seen.

"Nothing," Brenda said. "She's fine, Soph. You stay with her."

Sophie slid in tighter to her sister, her little fingers threading through Lily's. With Brenda taking charge of Sophie, he finally felt able to step away from the truck and jogged over to the porch where his mother stood. Her face was drained of all color.

"What happened?" He took her hand. Her flesh was cold and she wasn't even wet. He rubbed her hand between his to get her circulation going, worried by her non-responsiveness.

"A vampire came in." Her gaze locked with his. "You said you hadn't brought her trouble with her!"

He looked at the open door. "How did they find you?"

She jerked her hand away. "They didn't find me. They followed her. He knew who she was and became enraged when he saw…"

"Saw what?"

Brenda was suddenly beside him. "The other witch? You didn't mention you were expecting company."

Alandra didn't respond to her question. "I want you all to leave, now!"

"How do you know the vampire tracked her? What if it isn't safe for you here any longer?" He stepped between Brenda and Alandra to get his mother to focus on him.

"She'll be safe now," Lily said softly behind him.

Chapter 10

Alandra wouldn't look at her, but Lily couldn't say she was surprised. If she'd just tried to have someone killed it would probably be difficult to meet their eyes. Reyes spun around, relief clear in his gaze, but his relief would shortly turn to disbelief and then anger, most likely directed at her.

"Why?" she asked the one question she had wondered since finding herself tied to the chair.

Reyes frowned, his gaze going from her to his mother and back again.

Alandra didn't answer. Lily hadn't really expected her to. With a small sigh, she squeezed Soph's hand to reassure her. She needed to be careful of what she said, but she had a feeling a part of her sister had been with her the entire time. She'd felt her calming presence. It was something to figure out and deal with later.

"Brenda, you need to check the vampire's body." She locked eyes with her vamp. "It's the same one I killed two nights ago."

Brenda pivoted to look at the open front door. "You sure?"

"Pretty sure." His presence had felt the same as before even if she hadn't gotten a straight look at him. "If he survived then…"

"Right." Brenda was already running up the steps to make sure the master vampire was indeed dead and wouldn't come back to chase them again.

"If you didn't want me in your home, you could have told me to leave," Lily said softly, keeping her gaze on Alandra's face, but watching Reyes out of the corner of her eye. She was about to accuse his mother of trying to kill her.

Alandra's eyes narrowed. "You were already here. She felt your presence as soon as you entered the island. This is her domain."

Reyes cleared his throat. "Someone want to clue me in to what the heck we're talking about?"

She took a deep breath. "Your mother isn't dying, Reyes. She's being drained of her light by another witch."

"What?" He stared at his mother in dismay. "Why didn't you tell me someone was hurting you?"

Alandra avoided her son's gaze. "She wasn't hurting me."

"It certainly hurt me when she attempted to drain my light," Lily spat out before she could hold back.

Reyes winced at Lily's accusation and his eyes locked with hers. Her heart squeezed as she waited for what he was going to say. She hadn't flat out accused his mother of trying to kill her and maybe the two women wouldn't have killed her. She didn't know what their plans had been exactly. But he didn't verbally respond as his gaze went back to his mother's face.

Taking a deep breath, she tried to keep control as more of her power surged inside her. "She drained you over and over, didn't she?"

Alandra glared at her. "It was better than being constantly on the run from vampires. She made me invisible to them."

"Why didn't you tell me?" Reyes asked softly. "I always asked how you were."

"I was fine," Alandra said, her chin going up. "Why would I tell you anything?"

His hurt shot right through Lily's heart and she couldn't hold the words in. "Because he's your son and he cares about you. She didn't care about you. All she wanted was your power for herself."

Reyes stared at the ground his agony coming off him in waves. "You hate me that much?"

Alandra's stubborn expression turned to one of surprise. "I've never hated you."

Lily suddenly understood why Alandra had put herself through the agony of having her power drained from her. "You hated yourself."

"Wouldn't you? It was my job to protect my daughter - to guide her into her full powers and I failed." Alandra's gaze didn't waver. "I failed her and she died."

Sophie squeezed Lily's hand and she squeezed it back, dropping down to pick her up and cuddle her against the cool wet breeze. Her sister's clothes were just as soaked as her own were now. She couldn't say what she wanted to the woman with Soph's ears pricked and ready to remember every word. She kissed Sophie's cheek and tried to reassure her with a hug.

"I'm fine," she whispered in her sister's ear.

Reyes looked back to his mother. "You should have told me you were afraid. I could've protected you."

Brenda chose that moment to exit the house and nodded to Lily. "He won't be bothering us anymore. The witch has white light residue?"

Reyes was still focused on his mother, and Lily stepped away from the two and jerked her chin for Brenda to come back to the truck with her.

***

Reyes waited for Lily and Brenda to reach his truck before asking the question gnawing at him. "What did you do to her?"

His mother's eyes narrowed as she drew her shoulders back. "What you asked of me, to make it so the vampires couldn't see her light."

"By taking it away?" He was having a hard time wrapping his mind around the idea of his mother purposely hurting someone. "She didn't ask that of you. In fact, she didn't ask anything. I'm the one who brought them here."

"And bringing their troubles with them," she spat out, "just as I feared."

"I didn't know we were being followed." He had no idea how the vampire had tracked them, if he had.

She looked over his shoulder. "They will always be followed. You should let them go and take their troubles with them."

His spine straightened. "I'm not going to abandon her."

She brought her gaze back to him. "I thought you would feel that way." She shook her head. "After getting you away from white lighters you still managed to connect yourself to one. I just don't understand it."

He couldn't explain it either, but he didn't really want to. He had no intention of leaving Lily. "We have a connection. As long as I can help keep her safe I will."

"She'll never be safe. That was the point of the draining."

"Jeez. Draining." He stared at her dingy aura with dismay.

"You could have mentioned what you were doing to yourself."

* * *

"We should leave," Brenda said softly. "There's a car rental place down by the boardwalk he took us to."

Lily shook her head, sheltering Sophie in the front seat and watching Reyes and his mother through the blurry windshield. The rain had picked back up. "We aren't going to run out on him."

"We have enough of our own problems without tying ourselves to his. He can't deny what his mother did with you standing right in front of him."

She shot a silencing look at Brenda. Sophie was listening a little too intently to their conversation. The power surged inside Lily. She couldn't control it as it tried to find a pattern. Not that it had ever been particularly easy to control, but the pulsing was something she had never experienced before. She closed her eyes for a moment against the pain. Sophie's fingers touched hers and she opened her eyes to smile at her.

Her sister glowed. She blinked again as the energy of her sister's white light met the surging power within her. She recognized the light within Sophie. When she'd squashed her own power it had somehow come to her sister. She didn't know how, but there was no other explanation for her suddenly glowing sister.

She smiled as Sophie stroked her hand, instinctively allowing her new witch light to work on taming the power within her older sister. Lily wasn't sure how long it would take for the energy within her to settle, but it didn't batter at her as strongly as Sophie's witch light soothed her own.

"We're going to be just fine, Sophie Baby," she whispered to her sister.

Sophie smiled and leaned against her. "I know."

Lily's gaze drifted back to Reyes as he turned away from his mother and walked down to where Brenda had parked the truck back on the road. His gaze flickered from Sophie to Brenda before resting on Lily.

"Soph, stay with Brenda for just a moment, okay." She slipped her hand from Sophie's grip.

"No." Sophie shook her head with a frown.

"Just a moment."

Brenda scooped Sophie swiftly into her arms and Sophie sent a frightened look to her, but didn't call out again. They walked around to climb into the back of the truck and Reyes took the remaining steps to bring him to the open truck door.

"I'm sorry." His eyes were fixed on the ground. "I don't understand all of what happened, but I should have realized something was going on."

She shook her head. "You had no way to know how your mother had figured out to hide her light. It didn't occur to me she was volunteering to be drained by another witch."

He kicked his foot into the dirt as he looked at her. "You're all right? Your swirls are pulsing at a much more rapid rate and you're brighter."

It was her turn to look away as she tried to figure out exactly how to explain what happened. "I think I absorbed the witch light power the vamp had in him when I staked him."

His arm shrugged and he inched closer. "That explains it." He took a deep breath. "I can't seem to apologize enough."

"You've nothing to apologize for." She rushed to reassure him. He wasn't responsible for his mother's actions and it was she who had forced the idea of coming down to visit his mother so she could get Brenda to trust him.

He stepped closer to her; his hand raised hesitantly before touching her lightly on her cheek. "I'm still sorry. I wanted to ride into your rescue."

She smiled. "But you did and most importantly you kept Sophie safe."

He glanced over her shoulder to where Brenda and Sophie were probably sitting. "I'll always keep the two of you safe."

She felt her smile drop slightly. Brenda had been wrong about him not believing her on what happened. He did believe her. But could she really ask him to leave his mother who so obviously needed help right now. She couldn't stay. The master vampire's arrival had shown her location was compromised yet again.

He crouched down, his other hand coming up so he could cup her face and tilt it up. "I will keep you safe."

"Your mother," she started to protest.

He shook his head. "She doesn't want my help or my presence."

She cocked her head. "You want to stay and help her. I understand. Just as I know we can't stay. Where there's one vampire a pack is sure to follow."

"How did he find you?"

She shook her head. "I don't know, but I can't wait to find out."

"Have you ever?"

"What do you mean?"

"You leave as soon as a vampire shows. What if there aren't any more trailing behind? Don't you want to know how he found you?"

"We haven't felt it was worth the risk before." She looked over his shoulder at his mother's house. "She won't want us to stay."

"No, she doesn't. We should probably leave."

"We?"

His fingers caressed her cheeks. "I need to stay with you. Here or wherever."

"Hmm." Something inside her relaxed. She hadn't realized how afraid she was that he wouldn't want anything else to do with her until he said those words. Even if his mother had refused his help and ordered him away, it had to pain him to be tugged in two directions. She couldn't in good conscience demand he abandon his mother despite what the woman had done to her. "Then we stay together."

"Thank you." His lips brushed hers in a soft kiss. "We need to figure out how the vampire tracked you here. If you knew how, you might be able to stop the vamps from finding you."

She considered his words. They had never been able to stay in any place very long once she was spotted. She had always assumed the vampires randomly ran across her. But that master vampire hadn't just casually come across her for a second time. What if they were tracking her somehow? Reyes was right. If she could figure out how they found her maybe she could block them.

Sophie suddenly appeared next to him signaling their alone time was over. She drew away from him to smile down at her sister. Her arms were up in the universal pick me up sign. Reyes scooped her up before Lily had the chance and Sophie slid into his arms easily to give him a hug before climbing into Lily's lap.

Brenda trailed behind her. "Are we ready to go?"

Lily snuggled her sister. "Not just yet. After we clean up the mess we made."

The vamp huffed, clearly not surprised and not happy with her decision. "She won't welcome our help."

"She'll get it anyway," she said and Sophie nodded.

"Fine. I'll get started on the most immediate problem." Brenda paced back toward the house.

Alandra hadn't moved from her spot, but finally seemed to react as she shrank away from the vampire striding into her house. Lily pulled her gaze away from Alandra to kiss the top of her sister's head. She ran her hand through Sophie's ponytail as her sister's new light continued to sooth her own erratic light.

She had always had a magical connection to her sister, but to have her light go to Sophie in that moment such a short time ago seemed to defy explanation. Lily hadn't intentionally sent the power to her. Yet, it had somehow left her and gone into her sister when she had tried to stop the witch from taking her light.

Closing her eyes, Lily considered the implications of her sister now being a white light witch as well. They would be double the target and up to this point the vampires had never been focused on her sister. Now they would be.

"Hey." Reyes squatted down and she opened her eyes to stare into his. "You guys are safe."

She bit back the automatic "for now" which wanted to emerge. "I know."

"We're just fine," Sophie whispered, peeking up at her.

"You and I are more than fine," Lily reassured her. "Maybe once the rain lets up we should play in the sand?"

Sophie's head bobbed, but her grip on Lily didn't loosen. She hugged her tightly and met Reyes concerned gaze.

"I'm sure I can dig up some suitable sand toys." He paused. "Maybe a meeting on tracking and hiding later on?"

She relaxed slightly at his choice of words. He had remembered her comment to him about terms being crucial around Sophie. A discussion on how the master vampire had tracked her down to the Keys was definitely in order.

"Tonight?" It was her turn to pause as she considered what needed to be done in that moment. "What do you need us to do?"

He didn't answer right away, his head turning slightly as he looked toward his mother.

She kept her eyes off Alandra even though her thoughts were directly on her. "Brenda will take care of the uninvited guests. Soph and I could put the house back in order. Give you some time and privacy to talk with your mom."

He brought his gaze back to her and his lips curved. "Sounds like a plan." He leaned in for a soft kiss, resting his forehead against Lily's for a moment. "I love you."

He drew back before she could respond and walked determinedly through the rain toward his mother.

Her heart fluttered and her power flared. He glanced over his shoulder with a grin and a wink at her reaction.

About the Author

Angie Derek writes steamy paranormal romances and romantic suspense. The idea for *Witch Light* came to Angie in a dream—beginning to end. Some elements needed to be reworked or eliminated as they only made sense in a dream world, but she knew she needed to tell the story of how Lily and Reyes met and fell in love.

You can connect with me on:

- http://www.angiederek.com
- https://twitter.com/angiederek
- https://www.facebook.com/AngieDerekAuthor
- https://www.tiktok.com/@angiederekauthor

Subscribe to my newsletter:

- https://mailchi.mp/831502633f9d/angie-derek

Also by Angie Derek

Mafia Secret

Lessa Noelle grew up never knowing she was the illegitimate daughter of a mafia king pin. After his murder, she finds herself a surprise heiress immersed in the dangerous world of organized crime with only the guidance of Marco Santos, her father's second in command, to help her.

An uneasy attraction blossoms between the two as Marco searches for her father's killer. He tries to keep the realities of his life from touching her and an already dangerous situation turns volatile when a killer turns his attention to Lessa.

Universal Book Link - https://books2read.com/u/bzd0N9

The Beast's Redemption

A steamy modern retelling of Beauty and the Beast. Cursed shape shifter, Alexander Léandre, is resigned to his fate, but that doesn't stop him from hunting down the descendants of the sorceress who bewitched him in hopes of obtaining a cure. Belle Beaumont is used to men never looking past her curvy figure and pretty face. She dutifully agrees to befriend Alexander in order to protect her father's herbal company. A single touch changes all. Passions flare. When Belle discovers what Alexander is truly after and why, will she accept him for what he is? And will her love and family knowledge be enough to break a hundred-year-old curse?

Universal Book Link - https://books2read.com/u/mlE1oM